W9-AQB-336

9/2021

Roll

with It

JAMIE SUMNER

THORNDIKE PRESS
A part of Gale, a Cengage Company

LIBRARY OF CONGRESS CIP DATA ON FILE.
CATALOGUING IN PUBLICATION FOR THIS BOOK
IS AVAILABLE FROM THE LIBRARY OF CONGRESS

ISBN-13: 978-1-4328-7770-5 (hardcover alk. paper)

Published in 2020 by arrangement with Atheneum Books for Young Readers, an imprint of Simon & Schuster Children's Publishing Division

Printed in Mexico
Print Number: 01   Print Year: 2020

In loving memory of Elmer and Brada
— you gave me
grit and magic.

And to all the kids
living with a disability:
You are amazing. I'll say it again.
You. Are. Amazing.
Don't let anyone define you but you.

1
SYMMETRY

It's kind of hard to watch *The Great British Bake Off* over plates of Stouffer's lasagna. Especially since it's been in the freezer awhile — the edges are dry and crusty. But this is about all the cooking Mom chooses to do. She says she likes to leave the fancy stuff to me. Really, though, she just doesn't have the energy to think about fixing anything that doesn't come with directions on the box.

Our TV is so old and tiny that I have to lean in to see what Mary Berry is pursing her lips about. The bakers are making English muffins, and she's giving the stink eye to the redheaded guy who didn't let his dough rise enough. If I were on the show, Mary wouldn't have to tell me how long those muffins need to rise. Any fool with a Betty Crocker cookbook or Google knows to let it double. I pick at a shriveled string of cheese on my plate and imagine what I'd say if I could send her a note across the ocean.

Dear Ms. Berry,

As an aspiring baker over here in Tennessee, I'd like to tell you how much I love every single one of your recipes, but especially your Cappuccino Coffee Cake. I made it once for my mom, and she said both coffee and cake would never be the same again. I think she meant that in a good way. Also, would you mind sharing your secret to a good scone? Because down here all we've got are buttermilk biscuits —

Mom's phone rings and now I'm left wishing I had enough sugar to try another batch of scones. The only ones I ever made came out so hard, you had to dunk them in milk to take a bite. Mom hits pause right as Mary is about to call out the top three English muffins. I already know which one will win. It's all about symmetry. They have to look exactly the same.

Mom sets her food on the coffee table. She's barely touched it, but she picks up her phone and walks into the hallway. She says "hello" like the conversation has already run an hour long. It has to be Mema.

I saw off another bite of lasagna with my knife and review what I'm going to say if the phone rings again and it's about what went down at school today. But there's not a single scenario where I don't get grounded. Grownup trumps kid like paper beats rock.

Mom leans back in from the hallway and mouths, "Chew, chew, chew," like I'm five and still in feeding therapy.

I point at the phone. "Talk to your mother."

Depending on how Grandpa's been doing lately, this could either be a really quick conversation or a really long one. I take my chances and hit play.

I'm right about the muffins.

When Mom still hasn't come in by the credits, I push back from the table and roll into the hallway.

She's sitting on the floor with her legs

stuck out and the phone in her lap.

"How bad was it?"

"He locked your grandmother out of the house and called 911 to report a burglary."

"Whoa."

"Yes."

"Did the cops show up?"

"No. He's done it enough times, she reprogrammed the emergency button on the house phone to go to her cell."

"Smart."

"Not smart enough to remember to put out a new Hide-a-Key. She had to get the neighbor to break a window."

I can picture it: Grandpa whispering into the yellow phone on the wall about voices and eyes looking in at him from the dark. Poor Mema. I wonder which window they had to bust. I lock the brakes on my chair and hold out a hand. Mom takes it and stands up with a grunt.

"Nice."

"Ellie, you're twelve. Just wait until you're my age. You'll make all kinds of noises you never thought you'd make."

She tries on a smile, but it slides off. I hate it when she does that, pretends everything's rosy because she thinks I can't handle it. But I don't say anything, just grab her plate off the coffee table in the living room and roll on into the kitchen. I don't know the last time Mom ate a meal all the way through. I pop her lasagna into the microwave. If it's not Mema on the line, it's Lauren, my aide, calling to tattle on me, which — I check the clock — might still happen tonight, with my luck.

I'm not a bad kid, really I'm not.

It's just that anybody who sees a girl in a wheelchair thinks she's going to be sunshine and cuddles.

Sorry for having an *opinion*.

Sorry for not thanking my lucky stars you get to follow me to the *toilet* three times a day, and sorry for not loving the fact that someone else has to carry my tray to the table at lunch and that I have to wait at the back of the bus, coughing in the cloud of exhaust, while the wheelchair lift goes down as slow as Christmas.

I'm sorry for needing a little *space*.

But mostly I'm sorry I let the whole

being-stuck-in-a-wheelchair thing get to me today. I wish I could have brushed it off like usual. Then I wouldn't be in this mess.

Mom wanders in from the hallway and slumps down at the kitchen table. The microwave beeps, and I plop the lasagna in front of her. It slides across the plate like a wet sock, probably tastes like one too by now. She's rubbing her fingertips in a slow circle on the side of her head. I wish she would stop doing that — it makes me worry she's going to go bald. I push the plate forward with one finger until it's about to topple off into her lap. She picks up a fork.

"Chew, chew, chew," I say, and roll into my bedroom to finish my algebra.

It's almost midnight and I still haven't started my math. I forgot to close the blinds, and the streetlight outside is casting an orangey glow across the walls, but I'm too tired to drag myself into my chair and deal with it. The chair's sitting at a right angle to the bed, where Mom always puts it in case I need to get up in the night. Right angles. See, I don't even need the math homework. My current skills are greater than or equal to whatever problem set is due tomorrow.

I could probably use some solid pluses and minuses to distract me right now.

I can't stop thinking about what happened at lunch. It so wasn't a big deal until everybody made it a big deal. I mean, I get it. Lauren's whole entire job is to chaperone me from place to place, so when I pull a runner and disappear, it kinda makes her look like she's slacking.

But Emma Claire wasn't there today. She's basically the one friend I have at school. She also has CP. Birds of a feather and all that. But she only has a limp and can still play soccer. I tell her she's got a "touch of CP" and I've got the whole bucketful. We're not *close* close. But at least we sit together. And when she's gone, it's just me in my cone of silence in the middle of the cafeteria.

So there I was, sitting at the end of the row of tables and away from everybody else like a doorstop, and it was loud, and not the kind of loud you can tune out. And it was chili day. The whole place smelled like meat chunks. Barf. So I packed up the sandwich I'd made with the cranberry relish and goat cheese, which Mom says isn't a sandwich because it doesn't have meat, and left. I just put it all on my lap and rolled on out and down the back hallway that leads to the exit doors by the gym.

I sat in a little ray of sunlight that snuck past the dumpsters outside and finished my lunch, and then the bell rang and . . . I just needed another minute, was all. Except when Lauren found me, I *might* have been dozing in the sun spot and it *might* have been after too much "travel time" had passed for me to blame it on the chair. But I wasn't trying to skip class. Really.

The thing is, kids skip all the time, and yeah, they get in trouble. But nobody freaks out about it like they do with me because I'm a health risk. And okay, yes, it was maybe a teensy bit antisocial to go eat in a corner by the dumpsters, but sometimes it's all just too much. I get tired of bearing witness to everybody else's normal.

I never got sent to time-out when I was little. I think the teachers couldn't bring themselves to lock me and my wheels in the corner. But I wish I could now. I wish I could just declare a giant TIME-OUT from school and people and take a long nap in the sun.

I think about *The Great British Bake Off* again and how happy the winner looked, holding up his English muffins like a doof next to tiny Mary Berry. I bet no one bothers Mary when she wants to eat alone. I bet she dines like a queen. One day I will write her a real letter and ask her to tea. I could handle company if it were Mary. We would sit in easy silence and let the food speak for us.

Two days later I'm at school, sitting out front by the curb and waiting for Mom to pick me up. It's freezing. I don't care what they say about winters in the South; it still feels like a bucket of ice water thrown over you every time you go outside.

"You want your jacket, honey?"

Lauren stands next to me with one hand on the back of my wheelchair. I shake my head, don't look at her. I've got my backpack in my lap with my jacket inside. If I wanted it, I'd get it. I'm working too hard not to be nervous about this appointment to have any room left to make small talk with Lauren. It's lunchtime and this is usually her "Ellie break," but since the "runaway" incident, she hasn't given me an inch of space. I can tell she's ready to go inside to the teachers' lounge, down a Lean Cuisine, and check her IG. I hate it when she calls me "honey." She's probably twenty-five at most. I wish we could just wait together in the quiet.

"We need to talk about what happened the other day, Ellie."

I look straight ahead. I can *feel* her hands on her hips. She already called Mom yesterday, just like I knew she would. Mom cut all my screen time for a week. A WEEK. I wanted to explain myself, but I couldn't get the words out. I'd rather lose screen time than tell Mom the truth and have her think I'm "not coping," as she likes to say.

"Ellie, honey, you cannot wander off by yourself after lunch without checking in with me."

"I was going to class."

"I don't believe science is by the gym, last time I checked."

She should save the teacher tone for the teachers. I wheel around to face her and tap my forehead. "Oh, you know, little ol' me just gets turned around sometimes."

"Ellie, enough. You know your educational plan requires that I accompany you from the bus, between classes, and to and from the restroom."

"So you're saying I'm in trouble for . . . *going to my class*?"

That's the thing about needing an extra-special plan just to go to school. Sometimes it helps. And sometimes it's the leash you get tangled in.

For a second she almost looks embarrassed, and I start to feel a little bad for giving her the guilt trip when she's not even the one who makes the rules. But then Mom flies up in the van and throws the automatic doors open like she's at the Daytona 500. She's an English teacher up at the high school and has to use her planning period to take me to my doctor's appointments. It's always a race across town to the children's hospital. But we've gotten only one ticket. The other times the cop felt sorry for us. On occasion this whole "crippled kid" thing works in my favor.

Today we're on our way to see the neurologist, the "head doctor" who reads my brain waves. It's supposed to be science-y, but it feels a little like visiting a psychic and watching her pretend to tell my fortune. I'm trying my best not to pay attention to the worry that's doing laps in my stomach. This appointment is a big one. It might really tell my future, and I'm not sure I'm ready to hear it.

"Where is your jacket?"

Despite the rush, Mom has all the time in the world to look me over while I'm riding the lift that folds down onto the curb like a hand opening and carries me up and inside the van. It's like the world's slowest amusement park ride. But she doesn't wait for an answer, because I'm finally up now and locked in. We're already going to be late. And I'm secretly glad. If it's bad news, it's bad news a few minutes later. I watch Lauren shrink and finally disappear out the back window.

Mom keeps checking her phone. I

reach as far as I can and grab it from her.

"Ellie!"

"No texting while driving, young lady."

"I wasn't texting. I was *about* to text."

"Same difference. Same eyes off the road. Text who?"

Mom doesn't answer.

I don't know why I ask. I know who. Dad. Dad the lawyer who never calls or comes to anything because he's busy with his new family. Mom says he hopes to run for mayor someday. I bet he practices acceptance speeches in the mirror. The therapist Mom made me see for a while when I turned ten and started ignoring Dad's phone calls and emails said I have "unresolved issues." She said I needed to learn to "express the hurt" if I ever wanted to have a "meaningful relation-ship" with him. But honestly, it's been Mom and me for so long, I think I'd rather just leave him to his bright and shiny new family.

"He might make it this time," she says eventually as we pull into the parking garage and the radio goes fuzzy.

"Sure. Sure."

■ ■ ■ ■

Mom and I both know Dad won't be here. Even though this is kind of a huge appointment, epic maybe if it pans out the way we want, he still won't show. He doesn't do doctors or hospitals or sickness of any kind — which explains the whole leaving us when I was still a not-toddling toddler. Whenever he visits, I make a point to lean over and drool a little. This would be one of the "defense mechanisms" the therapist mentioned.

The doors of the hospital whoosh open, and a blast of heat smacks me in the face. The elevator to the doctor's office tower smells like hand sanitizer and toilets, and it makes me wish I were back in class, which is saying something. A family sits under the television in the corner. The man has a long beard, and the woman wears a bonnet. Their little girl has neon leg braces, and she fiddles with their Velcro under her skirts. I want to tell the girl that the braces aren't as bad as they seem, that she'll get used to them. And I *would* tell her, if my voice weren't caught on a tangle of nerves.

I stare at the TV for distraction.

"It's always *PAW Patrol.*"

"You used to love *PAW Patrol.*"

"Yeah, when I was, like, five."

"Well, there are a lot of little kids here."

"Which leads me to my point."

"Which is?"

"Why do I have to go to the little-kid doctor? It's me and a thousand seven-year-olds in pajamas with their Build-A-Bears."

"When you turn eighteen, you can go wherever you like."

"Six years and counting."

"Just don't count too fast, okay?" Mom whispers, and untucks the end of my ponytail from my sweatshirt. Her hand is shaking, and I lean into it for a second like a cat until it stills.

She looks back down at her phone. Still no text from Dad. I'm half thinking about what comes next and half still mad over my conversation with Lauren earlier, when the door opens and a nurse steps out. "Cowan?"

Both of our heads snap up like we're in

trouble. We take a deep breath at the same time, like we're going underwater, and then I wheel forward and Mom gets up to follow.

The exam room has planes on the walls in primary colors and a train rug on the floor. Who thinks this stuff up? Like making it look like a nursery means we don't know what goes down in here? Needles and tape and cold hands and stethoscopes . . . and hours and hours of endless waiting. I get my phone out to Snapchat Emma Claire so I won't just watch the clock. And she understands the doctor's office torture — the jangly nerves and ticktock tediousness. I peek over at Mom to see if she's going to get on me for being on my phone, but she either doesn't notice or doesn't care. But miracle upon miracle, before I can even hit the app, the door opens.

"Hello, Mrs. Cowan and . . ." The doctor pauses to look at her chart. "And Lily."

"It's Ellie," I say.

"And it's *Ms.* Cowan," Mom adds, but I don't think the doctor hears her, or cares.

"Well, it's nice to meet you, Ellie. I'm Dr. Reardon."

I can tell she doesn't like my nickname. When I was little and not strong enough yet to get my words to come out right, I couldn't say my own name. "Lily" came out "Ellie." It stuck. I'm not going to explain it to her.

"Ellie, I've been reviewing your charts and the most recent EEG."

The EEG is a readout of brain waves, and if you squint at it, it looks just like the ocean with peaks and dips. I glance over at Mom, and she's holding her purse tight to her chest like a little old lady on the bus. These appointments wind her up. She always thinks they're going to be doom and gloom. Storms at sea. And this one is the big reevaluation, the chance to see if I'm still as seizure-y as I used to be. I'm not gonna lie, I'm a little wound up about it myself. I wish I had something to do with my hands, something to hug, like my old stuffed bear I used to take to all the doctor visits when I was little. We named him Carl, after the main character from the movie *Up,* because by the time I had learned to speak, I'd already rubbed his ears bald. He looked exactly like a little old man.

"And it looks like there's been no abnormal activity in . . ." Long pause as the doctor flips through pages and pushes her glasses up her nose. "Almost six years." *Five years, two hundred and seven days,* I think, *but who's counting?*

Mom lets out a long sigh and slumps down a little in her chair. I kind of sag forward too and prop my elbows on my armrests. It's like the good news chased out the worry that was keeping me upright. I can see Mom remembering the fevers and the shakes and the ambulance rides from the seizures. That part's all a big blur to me. But the fear, like listening for the storm you know is coming, *that* I remember. I rock back and forth on my wheels, ready to get this show on the road. I've been telling Mom for years she doesn't have to baby me, and now I have proof.

"I think we're safe to discontinue all medication at this point, Lily — sorry — Ellie. It seems you have outgrown the seizures, as we'd hoped." The doctor waits for . . . what? Smiles maybe? Claps on the back like it's a job well done? I'm not sure, but when neither Mom nor I say anything, she stands and opens the door. Awkward. She doesn't understand that there's been mostly sickness and pain for us in this place. We don't know what to do with happy news in this setting.

"Is there anything you need?" she says, rubbing her hands with sanitizer, ready to get to the next in line.

They have to ask this. It's how we got insurance to help us pay for my wheels and the stander that looks like a hospital bed turned on its end. Just one note from the doctor and it becomes a "medical necessity." I hate the stander. It takes ten minutes to get me up and strapped into it, and then, you guessed it, I have to just stand there for, like, an hour. There's a tray so I can read or do homework or whatever, but all I ever do is watch the clock. It's supposed to make me stronger, but I don't buy it. I think it's somebody's practical joke.

"No, thank you. We're all right," Mom says a little shakily, and we watch the doctor leave.

"All right, all right, all right," I say to her back as we roll down the hall. "Right as right can be. Right as rain, thank you, ma'am."

"That's enough."

"What?"

"Don't be snarky with the doctor."

"Why? She can't hear, or if she can, she won't remember. We never see the same one twice."

"That's not the point."

"What *is* the point?" I say as we get in the elevator to head back to the van to drive back to school to live the other half of this already long day.

"The point is politeness. The point is courtesy. The point," she says, then pauses, "is that we've just been told you are seizure-free and *that* is a miracle."

I let that sink in — the idea of a miracle. You think of it like something you'd see on one of those evangelical TV shows — like if I'd suddenly jumped up out of the wheelchair and started walking while a choir sang "hallelujah." But I guess Mom's right. I guess you can have invisible miracles too, brain waves finally smoothing out and leaving me on a calm sea.

Neither of us says anything as she loads me into the van. When we hit the interstate, she runs the cuff of her sweater under her eyes.

"Are you crying?"

"Hush. I'm trying to keep my eyes on the road."

Later that night at home, I wheel out into the hall and lean way over to make sure there's no light under Mom's door. It's closer to morning than night, and even though I have school tomorrow, there's one more thing I need to do that's more important than sleep.

I roll as quietly as I can into the kitchen and use the light on my phone to sift through the bottom shelf of the cabinet closest to the sink. Tylenol, Advil, allergy meds, antacids, multivitamins, probiotics, and iron supplements. I have the medicine cabinet of an eighty-year-old woman. But I rattle past all that for the big, dark bottle with the childproof lid. It's sticky around the edges, and it takes a turn or two to get the cap off. The fake grape scent hits me like liquefied Nerds. It's why I never choose the grape Popsicle in the pack.

I roll over to the sink and hold it up like I'm about to take a swig. It's almost two-thirds full. That's like a hundred and fifty bucks, almost a month's worth of medicine. I very slowly pour it down the sink. The purple finds the drain in a thick swirl. Twice a day since I was six. Twice a day Mom had to use the dropper to feed me these anti-seizure meds like a baby bird. But after today's all clear, never again. I shake it until there's not a single drop left and then go back down the hall, shimmying my shoulders to a Beyoncé song no one but me can hear.

2
WRECKED

It's snowing the afternoon we get the next call from Mema. It's the kind of snow we like best down here, big and wet and so light it piles up half a foot in an hour. All the trees look like they're wearing mittens.

It's a guaranteed snow day tomorrow at school, which I'm banking on, since I haven't studied one minute for my science exam. "This is not a good start," Mom says when she sees me in the kitchen, getting out the mixing bowls from the bottom shelf and lining the counter with flour and sticks of butter.

But she doesn't stop me.

I'm aiming to make a fruit galette with peaches we froze last summer from the farmers market. I saw the galette in an old copy of *Food & Wine* someone left in the guidance counselor's office next to copies of *Parents* magazine and *Guideposts*. The galette looked nice, homey and fancy both, like a big fruit tart dusted with glittery sugar.

I'm elbows-deep in floppy piecrust when the phone rings. Mom is on the couch, surrounded by piles of blue books. The English exams were yesterday and she's buried in essays. She uses a purple pen because it's supposed to be more encouraging than red. I say an F is an F no matter the color.

"Mom." She doesn't look up. "Mom, phone!"

"What? Oh!" She digs for the phone, which she finds wedged between the couch cushions. She checks the screen and sighs.

"Mema?" I say.

"Mema."

She takes it in the other room, and I fold up my ball of dough in plastic wrap like a present and stick it in the fridge. My arms are already tired from the kneading. For the zillionth time, I wish I could stand and stretch. Because she's not here to yell at me, I settle for crack-ing my neck in that way Mom hates.

Ten minutes later and I'm sprinkling sugar over a bowl of cut peaches when she walks in.

"What?"

"What?"

"Why do you look like that?" I say, dusting the crumbles off my fingertips.

"Like what?"

"Like you've been hit by a bus and then backed over again."

"It's your grandfather."

I grab a towel to wipe my hands and roll over to where she's plopped on the couch. The blue books go sliding.

"What now?"

She leans over to pick them up, but then she just kind of stays there and puts her head on her knees. "He's in the hos-pital."

Oh boy. I try to swallow, but there's a lump of panic in there that makes me cough. This must have been a bad one.

"What happened?"

"He drove into Food & Co."

"What do you mean 'into'?"

"I mean, he drove the truck through the glass front windows of the grocery store."

Against my will, I picture his weathered hands on the wheel and see shattered glass and a tire spinning. I feel dizzy. When I was younger, he would hold me up so I could practice standing. He was always so steady. Something inside me topples over, and I wrap my arms around my stomach to hold myself together.

"I thought Mema hid the keys?"

"She did. He found them."

I put a hand on her back. It's knobby like mine. I can feel every bump on her spine. She aims her words at the ground and they fall heavy.

"They're keeping him overnight in the hospital. Apparently, the airbag did some damage — abrasions to his face, your grandma said. He also fractured his nose."

Ohhhhhhh boy.

■ ■ ■ ■

We eat the peach galette for dinner. It's a little soggy in the middle, but neither one of us cares. I don't think Mom even knows she's eating. Afterward she takes her exams with her to her bedroom. She works best when she's stressed. I don't. I spin in circles. Literally. I spend half an hour doing laps around the living room in my chair, trying to keep my body busy so my mind stops spinning. It doesn't work. Grandpa's hurt. Mema's scared. Mom's sad. It all sticks like gum and I can't pull out of it. So I give up and head down the hallway.

I should go to bed now. Or study. Probably should study, but my head's too crowded.

I pick up my phone, sneak into the bathroom, and lock the door.

I dial area code 918 and wait.

"Hiya, honey."

"Hiya."

It doesn't bother me when Mema calls me "honey." That's what grandmothers are supposed to do. It's a grandmotherly word.

"How's things?" Mema asks like we're just shooting the breeze.

"Really?"

"What?"

"*You* want to hear about *my* day?" I say.

"Well, I don't want to talk about things here. Honey, this place they've got your grandfather is a morgue. It smells like baby wipes and cigarette smoke. Lord, the amount of smoking that goes on outside this hospital, by nurses and doctors, mind you, makes you wonder all over again at the state of our health care."

"But you don't want to talk about it."

"No, I do not."

I can hear how tired she is. It travels down the line ahead of her words, and I want to reach across the miles and hold her hand. I watch the snow still falling outside and curling up all fluffy on the windowsill like a cat. We sit together in the quiet. I want someone to take my hand too.

"How'd neuro go?" she says finally.

"Good. I'm off the meds."

"Well, praise the Lord and pass the potatoes! Your mother must be through the roof."

"She cried."

" 'Course she did. Her baby's in the clear."

"She cried about you tonight."

"Well, she's a crier."

I don't tell her I want to cry too.

"Mema, how are you really?"

There's a long enough pause that I have to stop and check the phone for a signal.

"Oh, honey. You're a child. You shouldn't be worrying about this."

"Should is for suckers, Mema. You're the one who told me that. Tell me really."

"Should *is* for suckers. I stand by that, but this kind of truth isn't for young ears."

It kills me when she defaults to my kid status, because she's one of the only people who treats me like an adult. But I know Mema's in her own tailspin of worry, just like I am, so I stay quiet, waiting it out until she starts talking again.

"Baby, your grandpa's just about done me in this time. He's okay, but I hate looking at him laid out in this hospital bed."

And there it is again, another picture in my head I never wanted — Grandpa in a white bed, under white sheets and white lights, looking like a shell of himself. All those age spots from too much sun mixing with the bruises. I wipe my nose on my sleeve and clear my throat.

"I heard he found the keys."

"Yeah. I hid them in the pantry, but he got turned around going to the bathroom and found them."

I hear beeping in the background. It's steady, which seems good. And then a man's voice, muffled.

"Honey, look, the doctor's just come in and I've got to go. You go get some rest now. I'll see you in a week. Christmas, baby girl!"

She hangs up first. I stare out the window over the bathtub and try to see the snow instead of the pictures in my head. What you imagine is always worse. It's got to be. Because if it's not, if all the bandages and brokenness I see when I close my eyes are true, then I can't think how a person ever fully heals after that. Will he know my name when he sees me? Will he still look like my grandpa?

I turn to study myself in the mirror. Whenever I grumble about the freckles on my nose, Mom says I have him to thank. I tilt my head in the light. Brown-ish hair. Blue eyes that are sometimes green depending on the sky. And all those freckles that I will never complain about again. I look down at my chair. That's the first thing people see anyway. I had a pink sparkly one when I was little. But this one's black with purple racing stripes I stuck on to jazz it up. There's really not much in between — you get either My Little Pony or the kind you see old people wheeled around in at the airport. Will Grandpa go home in one of those?

I hit the lights and roll down the hall into my room, a Pepto pink from floor to ceiling that was awesome at eight when I picked it out and makes me want to vomit now. I don't bother with pajamas, just heave myself out of my chair and into bed, which is harder without Mom's help, but I don't want to bug her.

I try to let sleep take me. But my legs are doing that twitching thing they do when the muscles get stiff and I'm restless. Every time I close my eyes, I see Grandpa's busted face and I twitch.

Mom looks terrible the next morning. If she did sleep, it doesn't show. She sits at the kitchen table and picks at the fake wood that's flaking around its edge. It is not a nice table. Nothing in this place really is; we just like it because it's cheap and doesn't have stairs.

I hand her the orange I was peeling and grab another one. She takes it and we stare at the TV. The map of the middle of the state is whited out. The weatherman says I was right. Almost every county is out of school. But the snow's already melting, and it's more gray than white from the grit off the road.

"We need to talk," Mom says, real slow like she's about to tell me I'm adopted or something.

"Yep," I say, trying to keep it light even though I feel fear as hard as a peach pit about whatever's coming next.

"I'm worried about your grandfather."

"Yep."

"Ellie, be serious. I'm also worried about Mema."

"She says not to."

"You called her." It's a statement, not a question, so I nod.

"So you think we shouldn't worry?" she asks, but I can tell she's really just talking to herself.

"I think Mema's never going to admit how bad it is," I say, and put down my orange. I can't get the peel started right and it's coming off in tiny pieces.

Mom sucks on an orange slice. She looks weirdly better. Relieved maybe? She stands and grabs bowls and Frosted Flakes from the cupboard, then pours the cereal in without milk. We always eat our cereal dry, an old habit that's hung around from my early years, when I was allergic to just about everything, including dairy. They say it's normal for kids like me who were born super early to have allergies. I say, no, it's still weird, but weird is my normal.

After a minute or so of crunching that's

louder than the TV, she says, "What would you say to making our Christmas vacation a little bit longer?"

I want to yell "Yes!" because extra time with my grandparents always feels like a second dessert. Maybe this will be enough to really help Grandpa. But I'm trying to keep it cool, so I ask as calm as can be, "How much longer?"

"The spring semester?"

"For real?"

"For real."

"So I can quit school?" Dreams really do come true.

She raises an eyebrow at me. She can do this. Her eyebrows are like a cartoon character's.

"No, you can *transfer* to the middle school in Eufaula."

Oh. New school. New people who get to stare at the new kid in the wheelchair. The cereal turns to sawdust in my throat. If a kid can't talk well, I've seen parents hang a sign on the wheelchair that says, "Hi, my name is _____ and I have _____ and my favorite color is _____." It's like a CliffsNotes version of a person. Maybe I'll pretend I can't talk at the new school and do that. Nobody'd know the difference.

"Would you teach at the high school?"

"I called this morning. There's nothing available, but they'll have me on as a substitute."

"Do I have to finish my exams?"

"You mean *start* your exams?"

"Yeah."

"Yes, you have to start and finish, and then we leave."

Brakes squeak outside. The neighbor in our duplex is heading off to who knows where. Every week he pulls in with a new delivery sign on his car. This week it's THE SNAPPY TOMATO. I wonder if he'll give us free pizza. I think of who I'll eat lunch with at this new school when I can't sit with Emma Claire. Probably no one.

"Mema's never going to go for this."

"That's why we don't tell her until we're there."

"So lie?" I try to raise my eyebrow as high as Mom's but can't quite make it.

"No, not lie. Delay the inevitable."

"So stall."

She takes both of our bowls to the sink.

"Yes, stall."

"I like it."

The counselor's office looks like an ad for PBS Kids — there's a painting on the wall of a face with a nose on the forehead and eyes where ears should be. Every angle I try, it won't come out right. The room itself is all bright pastel, if that's even a thing — purple and peach and green everywhere, and a little lamp with a peach shade. It's like '90s Barbie became a school counselor. But Mrs. Lawrence is nice and always remembers to move the chairs so I can roll right in. She's sitting behind her desk, while Lauren and the special ed coordinator, Mrs. Hayes, sit on the couch along one wall and Mom stands next to me by the door. Fast exits are key.

"We understand your special circumstances, Ms. Cowan, and we are sorry to lose Ellie halfway through the school year, but our job today is to make sure we have a competent assessment of her current needs to send on to her new school in . . ." Mrs. Hayes looks down at her notes. Her purple glasses hang on the tip of her nose, and I wait for them to topple off, but they don't.

"Oklahoma," Mom says.

"Yes, Oklahoma." Now Mrs. Hayes looks at Lauren, and I have to shut my mouth so I don't actually sigh out loud. "What are your observations, Ms. Osborne?"

"Well," Lauren says from the depths of her turtleneck, "I think given Ellie's history, I would recommend her continuing with an aide at her new school."

We all know by "history" she means "medical history" — the thing I can't outrun. Cerebral palsy is like the "Go to Jail" card in Monopoly: No matter where you are, it always shoots you back to zero. In my case, that's birth, day one of CP.

Nobody knows what went wrong, exactly. Mom's water broke at a Fourth of July picnic right as she was taking a bite of egg salad. How much less prepared could you be if you're eating a sandwich in the middle of a field when you go into labor? You can't blame her, though. She was supposed to have three more months before I showed up.

It happens to a lot of really early babies, I guess, this cerebral ("brain") palsy ("paralysis") that left me different from everybody else. The brain just isn't ready to protect itself from the bumps and bruises of the outside world. It's like a snail that hasn't grown its shell.

The doctors may not know what caused it, but they know what it does to me. It makes it so I can't move my body like I want. It's like everything is both weaker and heavier at the same time — like your leg's gone numb, and you know if you could just shake the pins and needles out, then you could get up and walk it off. Or at least that's what I imagine, when I imagine standing and walking on my own.

It's not as bad as it was in the beginning, though. I couldn't eat or even breathe without help at first. I stayed with all the other tiny sick babies in intensive care for weeks and weeks. Mom thinks it's luck and a blessing that I came home on what was supposed to be my actual birth date. We celebrate both every year — the day I was born and the day I came home.

But what Mrs. Hayes is writing down now and what Mrs. Lawrence is nodding along to, thanks to Lauren's brilliant input, is that I'm still a baby. Never mind that I worked with a physical therapist to get strong enough to wheel my own chair. Never mind that the feeding therapist let me "graduate" when I could eat and drink on my own without dribbling food down my front or choking on it. Never mind all that.

Just one mention of the "history" and I'm back to square one.

I nudge Mom with my elbow. She can't let them put that on my record and stick me with an aide at my new school. I give her the *say something* look.

And she does.

She looks at all of those ladies in that room and says, "I think that's a wise decision."

■ ■ ■ ■

We do not talk all the way home.

We do not talk over a dinner of cheese toast and milk and shriveled grapes, which are the last things in our fridge before we leave tomorrow.

We do not talk until it is the middle of the night and I have to yell from the bathroom for her to bring me toilet paper because there's none on the roll.

She's waiting for me in the hall when I come out.

"How could you?"

"Ellie, listen —"

"Why should I listen to you when you never listen to me?"

"Honey, I know you don't want an aide, but —"

"Of course I don't want an aide! I don't want an aide because I don't need an aide!" I bump up against the wall with my wheel in that way Mom hates because it leaves scuff marks.

She kneels down in front of me so we're eye to eye. I stop moving.

"Ellie, we don't know what this new school is like. We don't know how equipped they are to handle you."

"To *handle* me?"

Mom rocks back and sits on her heels, and now I'm looking down at all the tiny lines around her eyes.

"Yes, Ellie. Handle you. I'm sorry if that sounds harsh or demeaning, but it is *my job* to protect you. It is *my job* to make sure you are safe and looked after, even if you don't like it."

I want to cry, but that would be baby-ish, right?

"It's not fair."

"No, it's not. None of this is." She waves her arms toward the front door, where our suitcases are waiting. "But we're all going to look out for one an-other, okay? You, me, Mema, and Grandpa."

I know I should tell Mom how scared I am to start at a new school. That it's not just about the aide. What if I don't make a single friend? What if I'm just the crippled kid all over again? I'm scared about moving in with my grandparents, too. What if Grandpa gets worse, or Mema says she doesn't want our help and we've already quit our whole lives to move there? But I look at Mom, and man, she looks tired, like she could curl up and sleep right here on the floor, so I just say, "Okay," and roll back to my almost-empty room.

3
ROAD TRIP

Dear Dad,

I'm writing from the road. Don't worry. I'm not driving (ha, ha).

We're on our way to Oklahoma, as you know. Mom said I had to email you and wish you Merry Christmas.

Merry Christmas.

Okay, now she says I have to say more than that.

Tap-tap-tapping because I can't think of anything.

Okay, how's the weather? Just kidding, we left ten minutes ago.

Really, though, I'm good. Wheels are good. See you in the summer.

Ellie

It's already been more than three hours and we're only just nearing Memphis. Tennessee is so freaking long.

I mean, it's not like I have a problem sitting. Obviously. But the DVD player broke last month, and there's nothing to do back here but watch the river appear and disappear again. If you've never seen the Mississippi, you're not missing anything. The M–i–double *s*–i–double *s*–i–double *p*–i is *ugly.* It's murky on a good day. In winter it's toilet water.

At least there's a big, beautiful lake where we're headed. If I play it right, maybe Mom will let me do more than sit with my feet in it this summer. Water is the only place my body isn't the enemy. In water I'm weightless. I can float free.

"I'm starving."

"Let's get past Memphis."

"But the barbecue's in Memphis!"

I saw an episode of *The Great Food Truck Race* where they went to Memphis. I want to go to Leonard's Pit, get a whole pile of their barbecue pork and shoestring fries.

I yell out the exit number at every mile

marker for ten miles.

It works.

We're back on the road in less than half an hour with greasy paper bags full of food. Why do barbecue joints always give you those tissuey napkins that tear to shreds when you try to use them?

Mom's such a pushover, but she's good at road-tripping like this. "Let's make it an adventure," she'll say whenever we have to do something half-miserable, like go for leg brace fittings or clothes shopping. Clothes shopping is the worst, with Mom following me into every fitting room and helping me try on jeans. As if *anybody* wants her mom to watch her try on jeans. But she somehow makes it easier. We'll skip school, take the day, eat picnics in the park or get Auntie Anne's pretzel nuggets at the mall, and take long drives with the windows down. She can spin anything.

I take a bite of my lemon square from Leonard's, and powdered sugar dissolves like cotton candy in my mouth. It reminds me of lemon cream pie. I remember that's what won the pie contest at Mema's church a few years ago. Every

51

year on the first weekend in May, Beth-lehem Methodist has a big fish fry and silent auction. And every year they have a Bake-Off and the best pie wins. It's kind of a big deal: there's a one-hundred-dollar prize and an awards ceremony, and everyone remembers who won last year and the year before, going all the way back to when the contest first started. I've always been stuck at home, still in school and wishing I could be there. I do some basic math — the Bake-Off is a little more than four months from now. I'll be there and I can finally enter. And I can win. I know I can. Every famous chef has to start somewhere.

"Shoot!" Mom says when a blob of red sauce falls on her pants.

I look down at my wheelchair tray. I forget sometimes that other humans don't come as well equipped.

"I've got a hundred bottles of beer on the wall!"

"Ellie. No."

I sing louder. We're in Arkansas now and stuck in traffic outside Conway.

"Take one down, pass it around, ninety-nine bottles of beer on the waaaaaaaall."

"Ellie, I will pull this car over right this minute if you don't stop that."

"Niiiiinety-nine bottles of beer on the —"

"All right. If you don't like my choice of music, you can pick the station."

"Anything but country."

"We live in the country music capital of the world!"

"Not anymore," I say, and catch her eye in the mirror. I shoot her a thumbs-up.

"Not anymore," she says, and smiles and spins the dial.

Two years ago, when we were driving to Eufaula for Christmas, the van broke down in the middle of nowhere. It was snowing. Mom's cell phone died. It's the one and only time I've ever heard her curse. She made up for it that day, though . . . aaaall the four-letter words. I don't think she knew I could hear. But she was standing in the gravel, kicking at the tire and yelling expletives for all she was worth.

After she calmed down or maybe just

ran out of steam, she put her hazards on and set out the little orange triangles she keeps in the back. She wrapped a blanket around me and put the iPad on the Nick Jr. app. It took her an hour and she lost her hat in the snow, but she did it. She changed that flat in the freezing-cold middle of nowhere America. When she climbed back in, we sat for a minute and listened to Christmas music while the van warmed up, and she wiped the black off her hands with wet wipes. It was nice after it wasn't scary anymore. And then we drove on.

If there's one thing I know about Mom, it's that she can do just about anything. I'm hoping that's still true. I'm hoping she can help Grandpa. Help him in the way he needs, I mean. Fixing a tire's not quite the same as fixing a person.

We hit Oklahoma just as the sun goes down, and it's everything I remember — flat as a pancake for miles and miles. The roads are bumpy with tar crisscrossing over the cracks like a zebra's stripes. My chair rattles in its harness, and I have to put away the book I'm reading so I don't puke.

There's no snow here, and I can see the red dirt edging up against the trees when we turn off the highway. It's big pines and oaks, taller than anything we have back home, kind of like driving into Pooh's Hundred Acre Wood.

We turn off Route 9 onto the gravel road that leads into Mema and Grandpa's neighborhood. When they first moved here after he quit his job in Midwest City, he called it a "retirement village." He said it wasn't a trailer park if nothing ever moved. And he was right. People here tuck their trailers up under these trees and lock them down with cement foundations and wood porches, so you can hardly tell where the wheels used to go. They build sheds and fill them with tools for their gardens and then fence it all in.

When we pull into 713 Alcoa Drive, the headlights snag on the smashed-up front of Grandpa's Ford, and it's so pitiful I look away, down at my chair, creaking as we bump over the gravel. Trailers. Trucks. Bodies. There're so many things wanting to move that the air feels electric with it, like when the hair stands up on your arms before a lightning strike. But I'm so tired, all I want is a bed and a blanket. If Mom's going to break the news to Mema that we're here to stay, I'll need to be ready and rested, because there's sure enough going to be a storm.

4
TRAILER LIVING

The first thing that wakes me is the squirrels. They're skittering on the tin roof and it's loud, like they are right in this very room with their claws clicking across my brain. I always forget about the squirrels. They're red, just like the dirt, and they're big as cats. You'd think in December they'd find a hole to snuggle in and take a break.

I turn my head and see that Mom's already awake. She's sitting up on the side of the bed and slipping a sweater on over her nightgown. Her short hair is smushed flat in the back.

"You only brought in one of the suitcases."

We were so worn out by the time we pulled in, we barely said a word to Mema before falling into bed.

"I know," she says, and stands to look out the window instead of at me. I grip the mattress and push myself up until I'm sitting and can see out too. There's a clear view of the Ford. The front bumper is hanging off and the hood's bent up like a tepee.

"And you didn't bring in my stander."

"I know."

"You've got to tell her."

Still she won't look at me.

"Mom, she's going to figure it out eventually . . . you know, when we *don't leave* next week."

Mom snaps the blinds shut and it makes me jump and sends the squirrels running.

"Ellie, I *know.* I will tell her in my own way when the time is right. You've got to trust me to know when that is."

"What's all the hollering about?"

Mema comes in with a mug of coffee and hands it to Mom. There's a mouse on it lifting a barbell, and it reads: LORD, GIVE ME STRENGTH. Mema's short, but she squints at both of us so the lines around her blue eyes multiply and she looks fierce, like a tiny army general. Mom sips and eyes me over the rim.

"Nothing, Mema. I'm just not ready to get up yet," I say.

"Well, you just sit tight, then, and I'll get the food going. No one argues in my house before breakfast."

She claps once and then holds her hands out like she's trying to hug the whole room. "I am just so happy to have my girls home."

After she leaves, Mom comes over and sits next to me and asks, "Need some help getting into your chair?"

I shake my head. Why would I let her help me when she never lets me help her?

"Here, mix these together."

Mema passes me a plastic yellow bowl and dumps in two handfuls of flour and one of cornmeal. I dig through the drawers for a wooden spoon and notice she's moved all the bowls and dishes down to the bottom cabinets.

She's gotten ready for me.

"You didn't even measure it," I say.

"Measure, shmeasure. I've been doing this long enough, I don't need a number to tell me if it's right."

Her gray hair is up in a braid as usual and then twirled in a bun. She looks like the grandmother in a fairy tale. Except her sweatshirt has a drunken Santa on it with Christmas lights that flash. It says GOD GRANT ME THE SERENITY in big capital letters.

I roll over to the table and stir. Everything in this kitchen is yellow. The table, the chairs, the curtains, the rug. Even the floor, cracked plastic tile, is kind of yellow. I love it. It's like sitting on the sun.

Mom perches on a barstool, also yellow, across the counter in the "dining room." This place is so small, every room just runs into the next.

"Dad!" she says when Grandpa walks in, still buttoning his shirt. She jumps up and gives him a gentle hug, the kind you'd give a kitten. His hair is wet and combed, and there are pleats in his pants. Standing alongside him, Mom looks like the crazy one, in her sweater and nightgown and troll hair. Except for the fat bandage across his nose, Grandpa looks almost dapper.

He comes over to me and squats.

"How's my little lady doing, hey?"

Up close, though, I can see the burns on his face and arms from the airbag. It looks like a really bad rash, and now I, too, want to hug him like he's a kitten.

"I'm good, Grandpa. Real good."

"That thing holding up okay?" he says, and pats the armrest on my chair. He always talks about it like it's a car or a horse.

"Yeah, it's good. Mom just let me take the stabilizers off. Want to see?"

I pull back from the table and rock backward so my feet are up in the air. It's not for more than a few seconds, but Mom and Mema gasp like I'm about to drop a tray of dishes.

"Ellie, that is not why we took those extra wheels off the back!" Mom says, and I drop down again.

"Honey, do not be doing tricks in my kitchen," Mema says, and swats me with a towel.

"You two stop fussing over her."

"Thanks, Grandpa."

"Here." Mema hands me the buttermilk to stir into the batter. Biscuits on my first morning beats dry cereal any day.

Grandpa walks back toward the bedroom again, still fumbling with the buttons on his shirt, and Mom leans against the counter and crosses her arms.

"He seems okay this morning," she says.

"Seams are for clothes. You just wait," Mema says. "Lord, I love that man, but he is set to give me a heart attack." She shakes flour off her front over the sink and takes the bowl back. "Now, twenty minutes to breakfast. You all get out of my kitchen so I can finish up."

There may be no snow here, but it is *freezing* out. It's going on night now, and I'm sitting out by the front door waiting for Mom to bring the van around because there's no ramp off the porch out back. The wind hits full force because there are no hills to cut it, and my dress isn't long enough to pull down over my knees.

Let's not even talk about the fact that I

have to wear a dress, with lace, to the Christmas Eve service at church. Mema insisted.

I don't mind church, really, but it's awkward when everybody stands up to sing and then sits down again. Up and down. Up and down while I just sit. And then there's the "Please take a moment to greet your neighbor" weirdness. There's always one mom or grandmama who talks at me like I'm two: "Oh, hel-looooo. And how old are you?" (really loudly, two inches from my face). "The things you do for family," as Mom would say.

"Psssst."

I whip my chair around. It skids on the front walk. I swear the sound came from the bushes.

"Pssssssssssst."

"Who's there?" I don't know why I'm whispering.

A girl around my age in a bright red velvet dress steps out from behind the holly tree. Her hair's so blond and big, it looks like a wig.

"How y'all doin'?"

"Who's y'all?" I look around, like maybe there's a crowd behind me waving back at her. When she takes a step forward, I shrink down a little in my chair.

"Aw, you know what I mean. Hiya, I'm Coralee."

She holds her hand out and I make myself do a quick shake. I wonder how old she is and if her mother did that to her hair on purpose.

"Coral Dee?"

"Ha! Nah. Cora-LEE."

She's not wearing a jacket, and her velvet sleeves are puffed up to her ears. How is she not cold? Maybe she's a robot.

"You're Lily, right?"

How does she already know that? It's like my wheelchair sends out the Bat-Signal for kids far and wide to come take a look.

"It's Ellie."

"Well, that's a riddle of a name, Lily-slash-Ellie."

She leans in, so I catch a whiff of hair spray, the kind that's probably illegal because it burns a hole in the atmosphere.

"I heard my grandparents talking about you and your mama. They spotted y'all's van pull in yesterday. Nice wheels." She taps the racing stripes on my chair.

"Who're your grandparents?" I say. I don't remember ever meeting her when we've visited before. And I think I'd remember.

"They live next door — in the trailer with the pit bull. Don't mind Daisy, though. She's a scaredy-cat of a dog. It's the cockatoos you have to worry about."

Somebody shouts over the fence and I flinch, but Coralee acts like she doesn't even hear it.

"What cockatoos?"

I try to remember what a cockatoo looks like. Is she messing with me? I wonder if these are the neighbors who had to help Mema bust her window. I'm about to ask, but the shouting gets so loud, Coralee huffs and says, "Whoops, gotta run. Come over tomorrow or the day after and I'll give you the grand tour. And hey, welcome to Trailerland."

"What's Trailerland?" I ask, but she's already disappearing behind the holly. And I'm a tiny bit glad and a tiny bit sad that she's gone, because on the one hand, meeting new people wears me out, but on the other, I'm alone in the dark again.

Mom pulls up in the van. Mema's right behind her in their nicer, nondented Buick. Mema calls it their "church car." Somewhere in between getting me buckled in and our pulling out onto Route 9, I decide I'm going to take Coralee up on her offer to come over. Because she wanted to know my name before she wanted to know about my chair. That's saying something. And I want to see if those cockatoos are real.

Bethlehem Methodist is a one-story brick building with a steeple stuck on the top like an afterthought, or a candle in a birthday cake. Everybody wants to shake the hand of the "sweet child" in the wheelchair in her Christmas dress. Despite the embarrassing meet and greets, I do love this church. It sits underneath a bunch of huge oak trees all shouldered together, and behind it there's a creek and tables for picnicking in the summer.

We make our way up the ramp on the side, and Grandpa claps the greeters on their backs like he's the mayor. I see Mema rolling her eyes.

"Well, hello, young lady. It's nice to see you again," says a woman in a hat covered in fur and berries. "I used to work with your grandma down at the bank in Midwest City." She's got bright red lipstick on her teeth.

"They sure do get big quick, huh, Marianne? Oh, not that you're big, darling. You're just a tiny thing. Not that you're small, not that I can tell. I mean . . ." She stops and lets the sentence dangle like the end of a rope. It's kind of funny.

"We'll see you inside, Evelyn," Mema says after a minute, and shuffles us forward. She leans over my shoulder and whispers, "The key to Evy is to smile and nod and nod and smile, and while she's jabbering, just sing the theme to *Sesame Street* in your head."

Mom laughs into her collar and Mema winks. They both look nice in their satiny dresses, Mom in navy and Mema in cream. "Regal" is the word, and it's not something we Cowans can pull off very often. I think I drag down our average with my racing stripes.

We find a spot in the back row so I can sit on the end. The sanctuary smells musty but nice, like the way, way back of the closet, and the pews creak with everybody shuffling into place. They've got candles up by the altar and big red poinsettias off to the side. I wonder how the pastor's going to maneuver between it all.

"Ladies, my ladies!" Grandpa says, finally squeezing past me. Mema tsks at him for dawdling and then straightens the hankie in his jacket pocket.

"Don't you mother me," he growls as he moves down the line of us, and it's not like any voice I've ever heard, but the choir's humming and there's a shuffling of hymnals and there's no time to think about it.

Everybody starts singing "It came upon the midnight clear" with about twenty-seven more syllables than necessary. I sneak my phone out from under my leg to Google pictures of cockatoos, but

Mom whips her arm out and grabs it from my hand, mouthing, "Not in church," and I mouth, "What?" like I'm confused.

But now the song's switched over to "O Holy Night," and Mom leans into Mema, and Mema puts an arm over my shoulder. Even though it's hot as Hades in here, it's also kind of nice in the glow of the candlelight. I sing a little.

When the song ends, the pastor comes up front and the choir files out. Only one poinsettia takes a nosedive. Pastor Clark, in a brown tweed suit and a little red bow tie, looks to be eight hundred years old. But when he speaks, his voice booms.

"Turn to your neighbor, and let's wish each other a merry night before Christ's birth!" He claps and it's like thunder cracking, and we all startle a bit and turn in half circles. I wheel a little backward behind the pew and hide behind Mom.

"So, Alice, you're looking well." It's Lipstick Teeth, in the row in front of us, and she's leaning too close to Mom now.

"Why, yes, you too." I can *feel* Mom trying not to lean back. There's about a hand's width between them.

"My niece tells me you're going to be substituting for us over at the high school."

"What's that, Evy?" Mema steps forward, and now they're all so close it looks like a huddle.

Oh boy.

"Mother, I just called the school to see —" Mom starts.

"Well, Marianne, I thought you knew? Spring semester, my niece tells me. She works over in the office at Lakeview Middle now. Got her secretarial degree just last summer. I told her it'd be better to go to a four-year up over in Norman, but who is she to listen to her old aunt? I said . . ."

Mema isn't paying her one bit of attention. She's turned her head toward Mom like a hawk eyeing a mouse. To Mema's credit, Mom does look a little mousy right now. I think she'd hide behind me if she could.

Next to me, Grandpa wanders out into the aisle just as the pastor calls for everybody to be seated.

"Mom —"

"Not now, Ellie." Mom takes a breath that shakes her silky dress. "Mother, I thought it would be best, given the situation, if Ellie and I came to help you out for a bit."

"Given the situation? Help me out? Who asked you, young lady?" They're still standing, and they're getting louder. There are bright spots on Mema's cheeks, and she's gripping the back of the pew like she'll pull it up in one go.

I can't see Grandpa anywhere.

"Mom —"

"Not *now,* Ellie. Mother, let's talk about this later, at home."

"What home? You mean *my* home that I have managed to run just fine without you for the last twenty-five years?"

Something's happening near the altar. I hear the front row gasp. But half the congregation's still standing and I can't see.

"Who did it? I want to know which one of you liars and thieves did it!" The angry voice comes from the front of the church.

I grab at Mom's elbow. I know that voice.

The crowd goes silent and shifts and I can finally see what the commotion's all about.

Grandpa's by the altar, holding a poinsettia under his arm like a football. My stomach twists.

Mom and Mema turn slowly, like clocks ticking, to face him.

"Who's the man that stole my wallet?" He's sweating, and swaying like he's still hearing the music. The pastor inches closer, but I'm not sure what he's aiming to do. Tackle Grandpa, maybe. I try to roll forward but I'm stuck, and I'm frustrated for the zillionth time that I can't just get up and shove my way through.

"Jonah, come on now." Mema walks up the aisle. She holds out her hand like you do to a strange dog to let it sniff you and know you're friendly. But Grandpa's having none of it.

He's waving the poinsettia in front of him like a sword. "Get away from me, woman. This isn't your business."

"Jonah, I got your wallet back home. You didn't bring it. Remember? It's tucked nice and safe in the dresser where you left it." Mema has one foot on the bottom step. Anything could happen now. I start to rock back and forth.

I feel Mom's hands on my shoulders.

Grandpa looks confused, and then he looks at Mema and back toward me and Mom.

And like a switch flipping, he starts to cry. I've never seen him cry in my entire life. Not even a tear when he tore his thumbnail off hammering rusted nails out of the fence. His crying hurts me worse than seeing all the bruises and bandages.

"Come on now," Mema says.

He takes her hand.

The pastor takes the poinsettia. But something happens in the shuffle and somebody knocks into the candles.

There's a spark, and a root of flame shoots up the side of the podium like ivy.

Evelyn screams.

Somebody near the exit pulls the fire alarm.

A man in a green plaid jacket — I

recognize him as one of the greeters — runs in with the fire extinguisher and douses everything and everyone: the podium, the poinsettias, Grandpa, Mema, and the pastor. The air's full of smoky chemicals and it smells like wet carpet.

Even though the fire's out, everybody files into the night in a cloud of smoke and dust. My grandparents are white from head to toe like ghosts.

When the fire engine finally arrives, it's got nothing to do but wail its sirens. Its lights turn the crowd red, then white, then red again. We could be a scene from *The Walking Dead.*

Mom looks like she's about to cry.

" 'Tis the season," I say to distract her, but my voice cracks at the end.

It works, though. She shakes her head and rolls us out of the spotlight and to the van.

"Too soon, Ellie. Way too soon."

5
Merry Christmas

Dear Mr. Pépin (May I call you Jacques?),

Jacques, I recently tried to make your Country Apple Galette from a copy of Food & Wine magazine. Only I used peaches because that's all we had, and you do say that the dish can be filled with any fruit. Other than that, I did everything just like you wrote, including using the wildflower honey.

And so, I was wondering, since I respect you very much as a chef and like the idea of a dessert that is "both beautiful and rustic," why did mine turn out so soggy? Was it because the peaches were frozen? Did I not cut the butter small enough into the dough? Sorry about the butter thing if that was it — sometimes my arms get tired from all that rolling and kneading!

I wouldn't bother you with this under normal circumstances, but I am hoping to be a professional baker one day, sir, and so I'd like to get this right. Also, my family could really use a pick-me-up and I'm trying to find the perfect thing.

Your fan and fellow baker,
Ellie Cowan

The thing about fighting with family is that you can't get away from them. You're stuck until it's fixed or broken for good.

Mom and Mema didn't say a word to each other when we got home last night, and Grandpa had forgotten the whole thing happened by the time we pulled down the gravel drive.

So basically, merry Christmas to all this morning!

It's cold and gray and brown. So much for a white Christmas. Mom has to help me every time I go to the bathroom here, which is just humiliating, but the trailer bathroom is *tiny,* like airplane-bathroom tiny. My wheelchair doesn't even fit through the door.

"Turn on the water."

"Oh, Ellie, I'm not listening."

"Turn on the water!"

"All right, all right."

There's nothing like sitting on the toilet with your mom one foot away behind the sliding door. Did I mention all the doors in the house slide? The whole place might as well have shower curtains for doors, because you can hear every footstep, every cough . . . and every visit to the toilet. This is why it's not a good idea to fight with people living in such close quarters.

"Will you bring in the bath chair?"

This is another thing I cannot do by myself here. Mom has to lift me naked like a baby into the tub and Velcro me into the bath chair, which is basically exactly what it sounds like — a chair I sit in in the tub, with a seat belt so I don't slip down in the water. It runs on batteries, and I flick a switch and it lowers me in like a giant Easter egg. At home I can at least get myself *into* the tub, even if sometimes I need help getting the straps fastened. But one of these days we'll get a real handicapped shower that I can roll straight into and wash myself. It's a tiny thing no one else thinks about, the privilege to wash yourself without help.

When you're like me, you get used to seeing your body as a separate thing. Leg one. Leg two. Muscles and hair and a heart that beats. It makes it all a little less embarrassing when people are always putting their hands on you.

Once I'm strapped in, Mom leaves me to it. I hear the floors creak when she walks back to our bedroom. She's hiding from Mema.

I soak.

Soaking in the tub is almost my favorite thing, second only to baking. The heat and the water stop my legs from aching. You'd think my legs would never get sore, seeing how little I use them, but they do. I lean the chair back as far as it will go and let my ears sink under and my toes float up. Now the world is an ocean and I am weightless and it doesn't matter that I can't walk, because I can swim.

■ ■ ■ ■

"You smell like bubble gum."

Mema's in the kitchen when I come in after the bath. She's making some sort of egg casserole that is nine tenths sausage.

"It's the only body wash you had."

She pauses with her spatula in the air. It drips egg onto the counter.

"Did you find it under the sink? That must be from when you were a baby." She sniffs me again. "Nice, though."

"Thanks."

She hands me cups to fill with orange juice.

Mom walks past us, right on through to the back door and outside.

"We came because we wanted to help, you know," I say once the door clicks shut.

"I know, El."

"We came because you need help."

Mema turns her back to me. She lets out a quiet sigh. "Here. Stick this in when the oven beeps, and set it for half an hour." She points to the casserole dish in the shape of a rooster and heads outside with two coffee cups. I peek out the curtains. I can see the back of both their heads and that's about it. I can't tell if they're talking.

But all the important talks in this house happen on the porch. So after the oven beeps, I shove the rooster in tailfirst and take my chances.

"Can I join?" I say, rolling out onto the porch. They both turn to me, and I'd guess that neither of them has said a word to the other yet. They look like they've been having a staring contest — both their eyes watery from not blinking.

"Oh, Ellie, not with that wet head."

"Listen to your mama, honey. You'll catch your death out here."

They're in the orange-and-yellow-striped patio chairs on opposite ends of the porch, about as far away from each other as they can get. I move to the old rocking couch in the middle and grab the arm to pull myself over. Mom stands to help.

"Correction," I say firmly. "I *am* joining you."

I can see my breath and feel the ends of my wet hair turning crunchy with cold. But I lean back and let the couch rock me. This has been my favorite spot as long as I can remember — this big old ugly orange couch with springs that creak, and jiggle you back and forth like a baby in a bouncy seat.

Mom and Mema blow into their coffee.

Mom starts: "Mother, I only —"

Mema holds up a hand. "Now, I know what you only, and I know you meant well. But you lied to me, Alice, and that is not how I raised you."

I shoot Mom a *told you so* look, and she does her eyebrow-waving thing at me.

"You want to help? You came to help? Then you say from the get-go that's why you came. None of this sneaking-around business. You hear me?"

Mom nods.

Mema nods at no one and takes a sip from her GIVE ME STRENGTH mug. She hasn't told us to go. Not yet.

My turn: "Last night —"

"Ellie" — Mema holds up a hand again

— "I do not want to talk about last night."

Now Mom again: "Mother, we have to. Ellie is just as worried as I am."

"Ellie is a child, Alice. Children do not need to worry about their grandparents. They need to be roaming the malls or falling asleep in class or tweeting or texting or whatever it is they do these days."

"I'm not much for the mall."

"Well, that's good, because we don't have much of one here. This place is for old people, honey. We've got the lake, the church, and a bowling alley, and that's about it by way of entertainment."

"I like to bowl," I say.

"I've already taken a leave of absence," Mom adds.

Mema puts down her cup and holds up both hands.

"Stop. I know you've already set your mind to it." She looks back and forth between the two of us. "But here's my rule: You get six months. That'll get us to summer, and then it's back to reality for everybody."

I'm not sure how she thinks summer is the magic cure for anything, but Mom and I nod like we're entering into a secret pact right here and now. I feel the need to place my hand on a Bible or spit in my palm and shake on it.

The oven timer goes off right then and we move to head in. Both of them have to help me into my chair because I'm so stiff from the cold. But it was worth it. I'm the glue to their glitter. They can't help but stick around because of me.

When we get inside, the kitchen is warm and smells like egg and sausage. Grandpa is sitting at the table with the newspaper and juice, and Elvis is singing "Blue Christmas" from the radio in the living room.

"My girls!" he says, and we go to him and it's all right. It's going to be all right.

"Thank you, guys!" I say, holding up my new spoke covers. They're big black-and-white whorls that swirl like a hypnotist's wheel. Mom snaps them on like hubcaps and sits back on her heels while I do a circle around the living room.

"Those things make me dizzy just looking at them," she says.

"I *love* them."

Mema and Grandpa wade through the crumpled wrapping paper to hug me. It's late in the afternoon now, and we're sitting in the glow of the little Christmas tree. When I say "little," I mean li-*ttle.* It's plastic and fits on the coffee table. When you push a button on the back, it dances and sings "Rockin' Around the Christmas Tree." Mema got it at Walgreens at an after-Christmas sale and swore she'd never put up a real tree again.

There's a beeping in the kitchen.

"That's my linzers!"

"Your whatzers?"

"My linzers, Grandpa."

He gets that blank look he had last night at the church, and I feel the hairs on my arms prickle. Everybody freezes.

He looks from me to Mema. Mema looks from him to Mom.

After a second of silence, he says, "Either my dementia's acting up or I have never heard of such a thing in my life," and then actually slaps his knee and winks.

I laugh. I can't help it.

Mema swats him lightly on the shoulder. "Jonah Cowan, you're a mean old fart," she says.

Mom looks a little shaky, but at least she's smiling.

"It's a cookie, Grandpa. You'll like it, trust me." I actually have no idea if this is true, because I have never made one before in my life.

But Mom let me open my present early this morning, and it was a new iPad from Dad. He always sends something fancy. I guess money is easier spent than time. But it saves us both an awkward meet-up and I get something awesomely expensive, so who's complaining? I immediately loaded every cookbook app I could find, and this was the first recipe I saw.

I'm in the kitchen stirring the marmalade while the cookies cool when Mom walks in.

"Your dad called to wish you merry Christmas, baby."

I don't stop my stirring.

"I didn't hear the phone ring."

I know she called him. He would never remember on his own. Mom holds the phone to her shoulder and whispers, "Just talk to him."

"Fine."

"Be nice."

"I'm always nice."

She rolls her eyes and puts the phone to my ear so I can still use my hands.

"Dad."

"Lily, sweetheart." He never calls me Ellie.

"How's tricks?" I say.

"What's that? I can hardly hear you."

I hear *Elmo's World* in the background, and one of the boys is screaming. They are three and five. One of them is always screaming.

Elmo clicks off, and I try again. "I'm good, Dad. How are you?"

"Good. Glad to hear it." He sounds like he's on a business call. I can picture him crossing talking points off a list. "We're all good here, too. The kids say hi."

Sure they do.

The marmalade starts to boil.

"How do you like the iPad?"

"It's great, Dad. Thanks."

"Good. Good."

One of the boys screams, *"Daddy!"* I hear *Elmo* click back on.

"Look, Dad, I gotta go. But, uh, merry Christmas."

I duck under the phone, so I don't hear if he says it back. Mom shakes her head but lets me go and puts the phone up to her ear before walking away.

I stir and stir until my arms ache. The orange marmalade is perfect and smells spicy from the cloves. I know I should taste it, but I don't really want to. I take it off the burner instead and roll over to the window.

I wonder if it's snowing in Tennessee. I wonder if Dad ever misses me. I wonder if he ever wonders what I can do now. I wish I could stop wondering.

"Heeeeeey. Knock, knock. Anybody home?"

The back door is already opening, and Coralee rushes in on a cold gush of air. She's head to toe in green spandex, like she ran outside in her long johns. And she's got a sweatband on her head, like Barbie Gymnast. It's green too, with sequins.

I cannot think of one . . . single . . . word to say to this.

Mema comes in smiling. "Well, lookee here. Is that Miss Coralee? I wondered how long it'd take you to come knocking."

"Merry Christmas, Mrs. Cowan."

"You too, honey."

"I came to see if Ellie wanted to come over."

Coralee looks at me. I can't remember the last time a friend asked me over. I look at Mema. Mema shrugs.

"We've done our Christmasing already. You might as well."

I almost want Mema to tell me to stay. I don't know Coralee any better than her cockatoos. What are we going to talk about? And that other question sneaks in — what if she only thinks I'm interesting because of the wheelchair? Everybody's staring at me, waiting for an answer or for me to move. Well, I guess it's either this or spend the rest of the day watching *It's a Wonderful Life* on cable.

"Okay, but help me with these cookies first?" I say to Coralee.

It goes much faster with two people. I plop a spoonful of marmalade on one cookie, and Coralee squishes another cookie on top, Oreo-style. There's a heart cut in the middle so you can see the bright orange of the marmalade. When they're all done, I shake powdered sugar over the top. They might be the fanciest thing I've ever made.

We lay them on a snowflake plate and everybody lines up for a taste.

Grandpa eats exactly one half of a cookie.

Mema eats a whole one but dunks it in her coffee, which ruins the entire effect.

Mom eats hers slowly and says, "Interesting."

And Coralee takes one bite and yells, "The cockatoos are gonna love these!"

Weird.

I take a bite and chew slowly. The cookies are buttery and chewy, and the marmalade isn't too sweet. It's exactly like the recipe said it should be.

They're perfect.

I look at everybody dusting the sugar off their hands.

So how come nobody likes them?

After Mom takes me to the bathroom one more time, quietly, so Coralee won't notice, I roll out the front door. It's maybe four in the afternoon, but the sky's already getting dark. I'm bundled up in a jacket, mittens, and scarf, but Coralee doesn't even have a coat. I don't think she feels the cold.

I make it to the end of the driveway before I remember: The street is gravel.

I look down at it like it's a snake waiting to bite. There's no way I can wheel myself on this. My cheeks are hot now, even in the cold.

I start to turn around, but Coralee's in the way.

"You forget something?"

"Nah, I just think I'm more tired than I thought."

"Well, hold these." She drops the tin of

linzers on my lap.

"We'll swap jobs. I'll push and you hold the cookies."

I want to say no. I hate it when people have to push me. But I also really want to see the cockatoos. I show her how to tip me back a little so it's easier to push, and we move on down the road. When we get to her gate, which hangs crooked by one rusty hinge, she leans over to look at the new spoke guards.

"Cool hypno-wheels," she says.

Coralee was not kidding about the cockatoos. It's like rolling into the parakeet cage at PetSmart. There must be eight or ten of them flying around the ceiling and hopping from couch to chair to table. With their white bodies and spiky feathers on their heads, they look like little punk rockers. Loud ones.

Coralee's grandpa Dane waves us in from his spot in an easy chair in front of the TV. Apart from the cockatoos, their trailer is laid out exactly like ours, one long shoebox. But they have towels on the backs of all the furniture. I look around and don't see any cages. I wonder if the birds are house-trained. And then I look closer at the towels and figure it out for myself.

Dane has a walker propped next to him, and that one piece of medical equipment makes me feel right at home. He shakes my hand and then pats the walker.

"I've got a bad leg."

"I've got two," I say.

He laughs a laugh that turns into a cough, and Susie comes in.

"What'd I miss, y'all?" she says. She holds a tray of sliced salami and crackers in one hand and a cigarette in the other. The cockatoos go nuts when they see the crackers, and she has to wave them off with her cigarette hand. The smoke hits me in a wave, and I swallow hard and look at the ceiling. It has yellow stains around the edges. Mom would kill me if she knew. Smoke's bad for my lungs. But then again, it's bad for everybody's, so what's a couple of hours?

Susie, Coralee explained on the way over, isn't actually her grandmother. But she's been around long enough, she might as well be. Susie has big blond hair just like Coralee's.

"Hi, sweet thing. Don't you mind these birds, now. Just swat a hand at them and they'll get out of your way."

"But they can smell fear," Dane says from the easy chair.

"Hush now. Don't tease her." Susie pats my hand. "You'll be just fine. But we'll keep Daisy in the back, just in case. Don't want her knocking into you. She's a fifty-pounder who thinks she's a lap-dog."

"Susie, put those crackers away. Ellie's brought fancy food," Coralee says, and pops the lid off the cookie tin. Powdered sugar rises out like a cloud.

"Oh, I love fancy." Susie takes two linzers and carries one to Dane. Her nails are long and glittery.

They chew for a minute, and I look at my hands because it's always weird to watch people eat when you're not eating yourself.

"Mighty fine, young lady. Mighty fine," Dane says, but he sets his down after one bite, and after a minute so does Susie.

"What a treat," she says, and walks

93

back over to us. "Now, you need any help with anything, you let me know."

I nod.

As Coralee leads me down the hallway to her room, I spy three cockatoos landing on the edge of the coffee table. They start pecking at the tin. At least somebody likes my cookies.

Later, Coralee and I are watching a scary movie that she has on tape, like actual tape, VHS. She says both the video and the TV were her mama's. The television is the size of a microwave, but at least she gets to have one in her room. Mom has screen-time limits.

The movie's called *The People Under the Stairs,* and it makes me wonder why people like scary movies in the first place. I mean, why would anybody *choose* to be creeped out? Halfway through, Coralee leans over from where she's stretching her legs on the floor and hits pause. I see her face and know what's coming.

"So, can I ask?"

"Ask what?"

"What happened?"

The million-dollar question.

She points at my chair, and even though the smoke smell isn't as bad back here, all of a sudden my eyes start to itch and I just want to go home.

"Nothing happened. At least, not like you think. I didn't get hit by a bus or anything."

Coralee just switches legs and says, "Uh-huh," so I keep talking.

"I have cerebral palsy. Something happened before I was born, or right around then, and the doctors don't know what. But whatever 'it' " — I make quote signs with my fingers — "was, it made it so it's hard for me to move."

"Huh."

Coralee doesn't seem weirded out by this at all. Which is weird.

"I can walk a little. But I have to use a gait trainer — it's kind of like Dane's walker but a thousand times bigger." I pat the chair. "This is easier."

"All right, then," she says. "Your turn."

"My turn what?"

"Now you ask me something."

I think for a minute.

"Okay. What's with the cockatoos?"

Coralee sits up now and crosses her legs. *Crisscross applesauce,* I think. That's something the physical therapist used to make me practice.

"Oh, them. Dane likes them, and Susie likes Dane, so she lets him keep them around. But they crap on the furniture and it drives her nuts."

I laugh into my sweatshirt and then make a mental note to keep them away from my chair.

"Okay, I've got another one," I say, feeling bolder now. "What's with the leotard? Are you a gymnast or something?"

She laughs and then frames her face with her hands. "It's part of the package."

"What package?"

"I'm going to be a star, Lily-slash-Ellie. A country music star. But I've got to be a triple threat — sing, act, *and* dance."

She hops up and does a backbend and then falls into the splits. She winks up at me with her hands on her hips. She's like one of those balloons at the county fair that can be twisted into any shape in the world. And I want to laugh so bad it hurts, but I don't because I can tell she is dead serious and I know what it is to want something big for yourself.

"I'm staying here with Dane and Susie while my mom 'gets herself straightened out' " — her turn to use quotes — "back home in Tulsa. I hear you're here to help out with your grandpa. He has old-timer's, right?"

"Alzheimer's, yeah." I hate even saying it out loud. But word travels fast around here, so there's no use keeping it a secret. Although I guess there's no secret to keep if you crash your car into a grocery store and almost burn down the church. I want to ask about Coralee's mom. What would it be like to be left behind, waiting for her to come back? Life at a bus stop. Is it better or worse than my mom always being too close?

"My turn again. What's with the cooking?"

"What do you mean?"

"I mean, nobody makes stuff like this around here. Where'd you learn to do it?

Some fancy-pants cooking school back in Nashville?"

I start to talk and then stop about three times. Why is this harder to explain than the CP? "No, I taught myself. Am teaching myself. It's just something I like to do. I've been at it ever since I could reach the countertops."

"Well," Coralee says, "I think it's amazing." She stands and pops her back with a loud crack before falling onto the bed. "And you can be a famous baker and I will be a famous singer and we can tour the world!"

And that's the thing I couldn't explain. Baking is not just something I "like" to do. I love it and I'm good at it. But I want to be the best.

When everybody else was playing soccer or taking dance classes, I did this. I hunted down recipes or made them up from whatever we had in the house, and then I'd make something that didn't exist before. Not everyone can do that — make something from nothing.

I think about the pie contest in May. Just once I want to be known for something other than my chair. I think Coralee gets it. I think she knows what it's like to want something different from everybody else. I think we're kindreds in the way people can be even when they've just met.

That night after Coralee rolls me home and Mom helps me take a bath, because according to her, I "smell like an ashtray and your friend can come play over here from now on," I think about what my life looked like just five days ago.

I don't have my own room. Or my own bed.

I can't take a bath or use the bathroom alone.

I have no idea what my new school will be like.

But Coralee will be there, and Mom and Mema and Grandpa will be here when I get home.

It's finally not just me and Mom anymore.

I've got people now.

6
APPOINTMENTS

Dear Editors and Chefs of the New York Times,

I made your Linzer Cookies with Orange Marmalade for my family over the holidays, and they came out perfect. Thank you for the detailed instructions, especially what you said about the chill time. I am thankful we had the four to six hours on Christmas Day to chill (ha, ha).

The thing that I wanted to say, and this is probably my fault, not yours, but nobody really liked them like I thought they would. I guess because you said these cookies would be an "instant crowd favorite," I thought they'd be gone in a flash, but it's going on three days now, and we've still got almost the entire batch left, apart from what the cockatoos ate.

So I do have a question, but it's not about the recipe. It's about the people you make the recipe for. How do know what they'll like? How do you know what to feed your "crowd"?

Sincerely,
Ellie Cowan

Despite everything Mom said about the smoke, I'm still over at Coralee's every afternoon between Christmas and New Year's. She comes over here, too, but I never know how Grandpa's going to be that day. Coralee has starting calling his dark moods "Al."

She'll text, Ur place or mine?

And I'll say Mine if Grandpa wakes up and showers and comes out whistling.

But if he's talking to himself and still in his pajamas at ten, I'll say, Al's here. Uber me.

And she'll come over and wheel me to her place.

On New Year's Day, though, he seems good, and so Coralee and Dane and Susie all come over to eat black-eyed peas and greens and corn bread.

"For luck!" Mema says, and we clink glasses of sweet tea. Her smile is wide, but she looks tired. Because you can hear everything in this house, I know Grandpa's been up wandering around in the middle of the night. Sometimes I'll hear the dancing Christmas tree over and over and over again.

Mom leans close and whispers to me while we're eating. "Tomorrow's a big day. We're going to get you registered for school, and your grandpa's got an appointment with the neurologist." I already know this. Just like I know that neither of those things sounds like the way I want to start my New Year, but I swallow my peas and nod because Mom's tired eyes are starting to match Mema's.

We send Coralee home with the ham bone from the peas to give to Daisy, and then we play dominoes all afternoon.

"Hot diggity, I am on a roll!" Mema says after three rounds of chicken foot. This is the only game of dominoes I know. You win by making as many "chicken feet" with your tiles as you can. They look like little pitchforks scattered all over the table by the time we are done. Mema wins all our pennies and dimes and then serves everybody her peanut brittle instead of cooking an actual dinner.

It's awesome. And nobody says a word about what will happen tomorrow. On my way to bed, I pass Grandpa in the hallway. He's leaning up against the wall in his pajamas.

"You okay, Grandpa?"

"What? Oh yes." He pats me on the shoulder without looking down. "Now, you all be safe on your drive home in the morning, you hear?"

He's forgotten already that we're here to stay. Will this be what it's like? Every morning reminding him what day it is and that we're not leaving? The peanut brittle hardens into a tight knot in my stomach, and when I'm finally in bed, it takes a while to settle myself to sleep.

The only way to get into the town of Eufaula from where we live on the outskirts is to take Route 9 across the bridge that runs over Lake Eufaula. I love that bridge. It's so wide and long that if you roll down the windows, it feels like you're heading out to sea.

The lake is why Mema and Grandpa moved here in the first place. After a lifetime working on plane engines at Tinker Air Force Base, Grandpa wanted nothing else but to sit in a motorboat in the middle of nowhere and fish. When I was little, he used to take me with him. We had a special little chair we'd strap into the middle of the boat, and I had my own fishing pole. It was red and had Big Bird on it. We got it at the general store for a dollar. We would leave before the sun came up and sit out there in the quiet. I was his favorite fishing buddy because I'd had my whole life to practice sitting still.

Catfish was the only thing we ever caught. Grandpa would pull them in for us. Their long whiskers would whip against the side of the boat when they came up, shiny and dark, from the water. I'd squeal a little if one of them brushed against my leg in the bottom of the boat.

We'd fill buckets up with lake water and take them back home alive. When I asked Grandpa why, he said, "You want them swimming until they hit the pan, baby girl. Then you clean 'em and fry 'em up right."

But every now and then there was a little one, and he'd let me keep it as a pet, swimming around and around in that bucket, until all the others disappeared. Eventually we'd take it back to the lake.

"Live to see another day," he'd say, and we'd salute as its tail disappeared under the water.

These are the things I want to remember. These are the things I don't want him to forget.

It's twenty-eight degrees out on January 2 and nobody's fishing. The lake is big and dark and still. But if I lean over, I can still spot the red buoys, like inflated balloons in a line on the water, that mark off the swimming hole.

When Mom and I pull into the parking lot of the middle school, I see it's almost full. The teachers had to come in to get their classrooms ready for tomorrow. Just the thought of tomorrow makes me want to hit the automatic locks. This school is tiny, like old-timey schoolhouse tiny, not much bigger than the church. It's brick, like everything else, and there's a playground next door because the elementary school is right behind it.

Mom clucks her tongue when the only two handicapped spaces are taken by cars without handicapped tags. She's called a tow truck a time or two. But today she parks along the curb and hurries to get me out. She's already got her game face on. It's her advocate mode, the mom setting she developed from years of fighting for insurance to pay for things like new shoes to go over my braces and fighting school for extended time between classes and fighting teachers who thought CP was the same thing as a learning disability. Advocate mode accomplishes a lot. But it also landed me with a bodysuit I had to wear under my clothes for three years to help me sit up straighter. It was white with pink stars and I hated it. So there is a downside.

Today as we roll through the double doors (no handicapped button), Mom's face says, *We are the ability in disability. Hear us roar.*

Oh boy.

But the problem, as I see from the get-go, is that there's nobody to roar at. There's only one person at the front desk when we get into the office, and she's knitting. When she comes around to meet us, I see she is short and round and red cheeked and kind of looks like a garden gnome.

"Hi, you two. I'm Mrs. Peabody, just a volunteer up here at the front while everyone's in meetings." She cups my face in her hand and calls me "dear." She smells like rose soap. "We've been expecting you. Let me take you on back to the principal's office."

Mrs. Rutherford, the principal, is a tall, thin woman, and when she bends down to shake my hand, she reminds me of Olive Oyl from *Popeye*. A picture of the lake hangs next to her diplomas in her office, and she has one of those big old leather desk chairs that looks like a throne.

"So nice to meet you both. How are you settling in?"

"We're fine. Just fine." Mom gives her a firm handshake and then pulls out a folder with my name across the front in huge block letters. She bought a label maker last fall, and I am embarrassed beyond all measure that she has actually put it to use.

"Good to hear. Give your mother and father a hello from me. I didn't get a chance to speak with them at the Christmas Eve service."

Mom blushes, but I don't think Mrs. Rutherford meant anything by it. She looks like someone who says exactly what she means. No more. No less.

She keeps going. "Well, as you will come to see, we're a small establishment here. There are only forty students in the sixth-grade class. One hundred fifty in the entire middle school."

"Yes, so I've heard."

Mrs. Rutherford turns to look at her computer. "And it looks like Lily —"

"Ellie," I say.

"Ellie, don't interrupt," Mom says.

Mrs. Rutherford turns to me. "Ellie, is it? Well then, I'll just put a note in your file."

Mom opens her mouth like she'd like

to add a good many more notes to my file, but Mrs. Rutherford is talking again and ignores the folder in Mom's lap.

"Okay, Ellie. I've got you in homeroom with Mrs. Tilly, and then you'll travel with the B group through class changes."

Mom jumps at that. "Yes, how do you plan to handle class changes?"

"What do you mean, 'handle'?"

"I mean, who will be her aide? Who will be there for bathroom assistance, and what is your plan for physical education? Is the cafeteria handicapped accessible? Are all classrooms on the ground floor, or will Ellie need to take the elevator? Is there an elevator?"

Whoa. Mom needs a little less coffee.

Mrs. Rutherford looks at her over her glasses.

Mom looks at Mrs. Rutherford over the top of her file.

I see my chance and back out of the room slowly. Neither one of them notices.

I could have told Mom after one trip down the hallway that the school is only one story. It's that small and I'm glad. I hated having to be one of three kids waiting for the elevator. It was always me and some soccer player on crutches.

I roll along, peering into classrooms if there's no teacher there. The bulletin boards in the hallway are already decorated for the Cupid's Arrow Valentine's Dance. I managed to skip my first-ever dance this year. It was part of the Fall Festival, to raise money for new locker rooms. As if I care about the locker rooms. I stayed home and made a peanut butter cheesecake instead.

At the farthest end of the hallway (there is only one), I turn right and find myself in the gym. And the smell hits me. Floor polish and sweat. Every gym in every school across America smells the same.

I'm about to back out when I hear the squeak of tennis shoes and freeze. Across the basketball court, a man in a red tracksuit is stacking wrestling mats. He sees me, straightens, and then jogs over.

"Lily, correct? I'm Hutch, Coach Hutch." He holds out a hand, but he doesn't squat down next to me, which I appreciate. We shake, and I'm glad, and a little surprised, that his hand isn't sweaty.

"How do you already know who I am?"

"Principal Rutherford wanted to let all of us, those who will be your teachers, know that we'd have a new student to-morrow."

Yeah, I bet that's all she said. And I bet they always have a meeting when a new student comes to school.

"So is Hutch your first name or your last?"

It comes out sounding rude, but I don't mean it to. It's a reflex. Teachers bring out the worst in me.

He laughs, though, and rubs the back of his head. It's shaved in that way guys do when they don't want people to know they're losing their hair. "Neither, actu-ally. Hutchinson is my last name. Jim is my first."

"Well, I go by Ellie."

"All right, Ellie. Good to know."

I start to rock back and forth. It's a thing I do when I'm fidgety. Mom hates it.

"Well, Ellie, I better get back to these mats. I'll see you tomorrow."

Mr. Hutchinson, Hutch, turns with a wave, and I head back toward the office. PE back home meant private sessions with the school's physical therapist — lots of stretching on yoga balls and torture in the gait trainer. What's it going to mean here? Hutch seems nice enough and all, but do they actually expect me to change for gym? Am I supposed to play dodgeball?

When I meet Mom outside the office and we go back out into the cold, she's shaking her head and there are now sticky notes on top of her file in a rainbow of colors.

"They've never had to do an individualized plan before for someone with a physical disability. Can you believe that?"

In this school, yes, I can.

"But they're making one for you. Mrs. Rutherford's tough, but I think she'll fight for you."

We get to the van and there's a parking ticket on it. Mom looks at it for about three seconds and then she rips it in half.

"Mom, stop! You can't do that!"

While she's buckling me in, I add, "And not everything has to be a fight."

She looks me in the eye. "But I need you safe. I need you healthy, happy, and safe."

There it is again. Her favorite saying.

"I *am* healthy and safe."

"What about happy?"

"TBD."

She gets in the front seat and studies me in the rearview mirror. She looks so *serious* I can't stand it.

"Just kidding, Mom! JK! JK! I'm just messing with you."

She shakes her head and starts counting things off on her fingers. "All the classes are on the first floor."

"I know."

"And you are required to be present for gym class. But we're still figuring out what that looks like. Mr. Hutchinson will be your gym teacher, and I've got a phone call scheduled with him in the morning after I drop you off."

"What do you mean, when you drop

me off?" I thought I was riding the bus.

We've left the school behind and Mom is already speeding. Because of all her negotiating, we're going to be late for Grandpa's doctor's appointment.

"According to zoning codes, the bus can't go any farther down Route 9 than the entrance to Royal Oaks."

The main road in Royal Oaks is half a mile long and gravel, and Alcoa Drive, our street, is at the far end. She doesn't have to say anything else, but she does. "And they don't have a lift."

I lean all the way over and put my head on my knees. I've visited this town my whole life, and this is the first time I've felt like an outsider. Lakeview Middle might as well be another planet.

"Hey! Put your shoulder strap on and stop moping. Coralee's going to ride with you. I already called Dane and Susie."

"Great."

But I don't lift my head again until I feel the van slow. Neurology, here we come.

■ ■ ■ ■

Unlike in the school parking lot, there are rows and rows of handicapped spots at the hospital. As we roll toward admittance, I think how weird it is, going to see a neurologist, or any doctor really, that's not for me.

I wish it felt nicer.

Mema and Grandpa have both dressed up in their church clothes. Every single time I see Mema in pantyhose, it makes me think of church and funerals. I can't bear to think of either. I want to go back to the trailer and bake a giant batch of oatmeal butterscotch cookies.

When we make it past the receptionist, Mom is out of breath and her hair's standing up like a Muppet. We are *so* late.

The room they lead us to isn't like any exam room I've ever seen. It's more like an office, with a big polished desk and a print of sunflowers on the wall, which beats the airplanes and train carpet at the kids' hospital by a mile.

Mema glances up when we come in,

and she looks wrung out, like someone took her by her lace collar and shook her. A doctor in a suit and white coat stands and holds out a hand. He looks twelve. Okay, maybe not twelve, but young, real young. I have no idea where Grandpa is.

"Sorry we're late, Mother," Mom says to Mema.

"It's all right, honey. Your dad's just getting dressed. Dr. Hirschman was filling me in."

Mom turns to him. "Alice. Alice Cowan." Like she's James Bond. "I'd appreciate if you'd catch me up."

"Alice. Yes. I was just telling your mother that Jonah seems to be in peak form. Other than the nose fracture, he is in perfect health . . . physically."

We all take in the long pause before "physically." I am familiar with the long pause. It never comes before anything good. I grip my armrests.

"But?" Mom says.

"But," Dr. Hirschman says, "the Alzheimer's is progressing. Faster than we'd anticipated." He stops and looks every single one of us in the eye. "There are some decisions that need to be made."

Mom grabs Mema's hand and takes a seat. I roll behind them and bump into Mom's chair, trying to get closer. We are a sad circle.

"What kind of decisions?" Mom asks, all quiet like a little girl. I miss her take-charge James Bond voice.

"In regard to whether Mr. Cowan might need to be moved to a facility that can better meet his needs."

A facility. I know what that means. It's a fancy word for an old folks' home. It'll swap his sawdust smell with disinfectant. I want to throw something, but Mema gets there first.

"Meet his needs better than his own home? With his own family?" Mema taps the doctor's desk with her fist on "home" and "family."

Dr. Hirschman nods.

"Given the recent accident and the incident at the church, there are things to be considered." He steeples his fingers. They are long and smooth. The smooth-ness bothers me. He's too young to be playing with people's lives. Like, what could he possibly know about all this? "Things like whether he is a danger to himself or others."

Mema puts her hands back in her lap and looks down.

"Not yet."

"What's that, ma'am?"

Mema looks up. "I said, *not yet.* I am not ready to give up on him. I have been married to that man for almost fifty years, and we've been through the wringer, I will tell you." She points a finger at him like he's trying to call a bluff. "I meant it when I said 'in sickness and in health.' And I'll know quitting time when I see it. This isn't it." Her voice breaks at the end. "I got my girl here now. My girls."

Mema reaches back and fumbles for both our hands.

I roll forward as far as I can. I wish I could bulldoze my way right through this wall and this hospital and take Mom and Mema and Grandpa with me. We wouldn't stop until we hit the ocean. This can't be reality. It can't. Doctors don't know everything.

Dr. Hirschman steeples his fingers again and sighs.

"Mr. Cowan is seventy years old and healthy. There's a good chance he could live ten, twenty more years while his mind continues to deteriorate. Are you prepared for that?"

Mema stands and puts her hand on the doorknob.

"Doctor. We are all of us deteriorating," she says, and opens the door. "We might as well do it together."

Mom gets up like she's going to follow, but turns to me instead and says, "Ellie, you go with your grandmother. I'll be out in one second."

"Alice, what are you doing?"

"I'll be out in a minute, Mother."

I can't read Mom's face. But I can read Mema's. It's the angry emoji times a million. Mad is better than sad, though. At least for right now. I want to tell her that Mom's a genius at the work-around. Maybe she'll come up with something the doctor has never considered. I pull on Mema's hand a little until she starts moving again.

Back out front, we spot Grandpa in the waiting area talking to a little girl wearing an Elsa dress. They're standing in front of the fish tank. We move toward them.

"Your mother is trying to kill me, Ellie," Mema says angrily.

"Nah. She has her methods. I bet she's just giving that doctor a piece of her mind." At least, I hope so.

Grandpa turns when he sees us coming. He's neat and tidy and smiling. He looks like himself, healthy and strong. He looks happy.

"Marianne, look who I found in reception!"

We both look at the girl, and I wonder if I am supposed to know her too, but Mema looks just as confused as me.

"Look, M, it's little Lily! Can you believe our baby granddaughter has finally learned to walk?" He claps his hands together. "It's a miracle!"

Time stops.

And then it starts again.

And I am rolling on by now.

Past the fish and the girl.

Past my grandmother, gently taking my grandfather by the elbow.

Into the hallway where windows overlook the parking lot.

I catch sight of myself in their reflection and cannot remember when I started to cry.

It's way past lunchtime when we leave the hospital, and I haven't eaten anything since a rushed bowl of oatmeal this morning, but my stomach feels sloshy and heavy, like I drank too much water.

I don't look at Grandpa as Mema walks him out to the Buick and Mom loads me into the van.

When we pull onto Route 9, all I want to do is go home and crawl into bed . . . and wake up in Nashville. But instead of crossing the bridge that will take us back across the lake, we head toward town.

"Where are we going?"

"One more stop, baby, I promise, and then home."

I lean my head against the cold window.

Maybe Grandpa has it right. It'd be nice to forget your life. It's why I like to bake. When you're doing something that takes all your brain power, the world kind of falls away and leaves you alone. You can be anyone anywhere when your mind is so full of an idea. Maybe that's what Alzheimer's is — a thing that fills your mind so full of a story that the real world can't get in. Except that's a scary thought if you don't get to pick the plot.

By the time we pull in to Food & Co., I can tell I've been in my chair too long. My legs ache and I can feel the seat rubbing a bruise into my tailbone.

There's a crisscrossing of yellow tape over the front window of the store. And the brick along the bottom is all toppled over. It looks like a crime scene. Which I guess it is.

"What are we doing here?"

"Damage control," Mom mutters as the streetlights flicker on in the darkness of the gray afternoon.

Ever since I got my first pink wheelchair at four and began to notice all the things I could and couldn't reach, Food & Co. has been my favorite place. It's like a crippled kid's dream. Everything's set out in barrels and low shelves and little round tables. Orange and pink and yellow taffy sits in a huge bucket by the register, and homemade sausage biscuits stay warm all day in their plastic wrap under the heat lamps. If you swing by the deli, you can always beg free samples of cheese, and the bakery will give you free fudge, without nuts, which everybody knows is the best. It's like the original version of Cracker Barrel.

Today we go straight to customer service, which is actually just a desk next to the stand where they sell stamps and boxes for mailing. Mr. Akers is there, as always. I know he's a good bit younger than Grandpa, but his hair's completely white and he wears glasses that take up half his face. He is the friendly owl you might meet in the forest. He smiles at us now, even though we're related to the man who wrecked his window.

"Well, Ellie Cowan, you are a vision!"

"Hi, Mr. Akers."

He claps his hands and rubs them together like he's warming them up, before holding one out to shake.

"And how are you, Alice?"

"How are *you,* Walter?"

Mom does this, answers a question with a question, when she's getting ready to make a point. I think it was part of her teacher training.

"Well now, we, uh, had a bit of a run-in, as you well know. How's Jonah? How's his nose?"

"That's what I came to speak with you about." Mom pulls him off to the side, around behind the stamp stand.

Suddenly I'm starving. My stomach gurgles and I can feel it all the way down to my toes. I go searching for the sausage biscuits and grab a package of Hostess CupCakes on the way. The *New York Times* chefs wouldn't approve, but I love how, if you're real careful, you can pull the squiggle off the top in one long line.

There's a table near the meat counter, and it's set up with a red checkered tablecloth and a vase of fake daisies. It's a display for Miss Daisy's Home Cookin', a local catering company, which everybody knows is Daisy Alcott from down the street, whose husband died two years ago and so she needs something to do with her hands. I set my food down next to a case of pimento cheese. That's the kind of place this is. You can just grab stuff and eat it in the middle of the store, and nobody thinks you're stealing or tries to page your mom over the intercom.

"You are very attractive."

I choke on a piece of sausage and look up to see a kid standing in front of me with his arms crossed over a white apron, and — *is that blood on it?*

"Excuse me?"

"I said, 'You are very attractive.' At least" — he pauses and, I swear to you, looks me up and down — "your averages come out right."

He takes the chair opposite me. He's got hair as black as Harry Potter's, but with none of the charm. I look around to see if I'm being watched. This has to be a joke, right?

"Uh, so am I attractive or average?"

He blinks at me and then blinks again, and it's like the computer's spinning wheel — like he's uploading information and I am just going to have to wait it out.

I crumple my trash and start to look for an easy exit.

"Both. According to researchers, it's often the most average, or symmetrical, faces that are most appealing."

"Uh-huh."

I act all put out, but I kind of get that. People like ordinary — even numbers, even teeth, average height and intelligence. But in my experience, nobody would call a girl in a wheelchair attractive unless he was messing with her.

He's still blinking at me. That *is* blood on his apron. His name tag says BERT. I wonder if he works here or if he just snuck in to butcher something. A scene flashes back from *The People Under the Stairs* and I shiver.

"All right, then. Well, I think I hear my mom. Catch you later."

He just stands and holds out an arm that says, *After you, miss.*

I can feel his eyes on me when I leave.

"There you are!" Mom is standing at the front holding a ginormous bag of groceries. I pull the food wrappers from my pocket, and she rolls her eyes but hands me some cash. I run them through self-checkout and think how weird it is to hear the same automated voice from the Publix at home say "Please take your receipt" here at Food & Co.

"Where were you?" Mom asks as I follow her out to the car.

"Getting verbally harassed."

"What?"

"Relax. I'm kidding. Sort of. I think. It was just a really creepy kid. Or employee. Whatever. He had a name tag like he works here."

"Was he around your age?"

"Yeah?"

"Was his name Robert?"

"No. Oh wait. Yes? His name tag said 'Bert.' Why are you laughing?"

Mom doesn't say anything until we get to the van.

"Well, it looks like you just met your fellow carpooler. That's Bert Akers, Mr. Akers's son. He'll be riding to school with you and Coralee too."

"No. No. No, no, no, no."

After she stops laughing, I make her

explain. Apparently, Mr. Akers has about a million kids. But I guess Bert is the youngest and everybody else is grown and gone. So Mr. and Mrs. Akers live over in Royal Oaks now too, and Mom, because she is a crazy person, offered to give him a ride so he wouldn't have to take the bus.

If your name is Robert, why in the world would you go by Bert? Why not Rob or Bob or Bobby, even? Unless you're one thousand years old or on *Sesame Street,* it proves you are beyond bizarre. These are all the things I do not say to Mom as we cross back over the bridge on Route 9.

What I do ask is the obvious. "Why can't he just ride the bus like everybody else? He's got two good legs."

"I think he's been having a rough time on the bus with some kids from school."

I think about our strange conversation and the blinking thing. I can totally see this. He's probably on the spectrum. But I bet he's never been tested. I bet they hear "spectrum" here and think colors of the rainbow, not autism. And the bus is probably where all the bullying happens.

It makes sense; there's only one adult and a busload of un-seat-belted kids, and that adult is supposed to keep both eyes on the road. That bullying never really happened to me, though. Everybody who rode the short bus was in it together. We had to save our strength for the school day.

"I still don't get it."

Mom brakes a little too hard.

"Look, Ellie, Mr. Akers was kind enough not to press charges against your grandfather, who was driving with a revoked license, and he also agreed to split the cost for repairs. Taking Bert to school is the least we can do."

I see how Mom is trying to place Band-Aids over all the broken people. It's what she does. But today, after the school visit and the hospital visit, I just can't handle it. We have enough pieces to put together in our own lives without adding more.

"Oh, *I* get it. You're going to fix all the crazy people now, right?"

Mom pulls the car over so fast, the seat belt cuts into my shoulder.

"Do not —" she says, and takes a

breath and turns around to look at me, "*ever* call your grandfather crazy. He is sick and we are here to help him. And as for Bert, I think you should try to be a little more open-minded. Empathy and sympathy, Ellie. That's what we all need. Empathy and sympathy."

"Fine." I point to the road. "Can we go now?" I don't want the lecture. I just want to get out of here and forget this day ever happened.

She sighs but pulls back into the lane. I can see her knuckles white on the wheel, like she could crack the thing in two. I think about Grandpa clapping his hands over the little "walking Ellie" at the hospital. I think about what it means to be attractive and how I will never be.

Empathy and sympathy. I'm just fresh out.

7
FALSE START

"I am never going back."

"Honey, you have to tell me what happened."

Mom is sitting next to me in our bedroom. I've pulled myself onto the bed, but I'm too tired to drag the quilt over me. It's yellow and covered in girls in bonnets. From this angle, it looks like they're little Pac-Mans about to attack my legs — my skinny, stupid, useless legs.

"Please. I can't make it better if I don't know."

Mom smooths the hair back from my forehead and pulls the cuffs of my jeans down where they were bunched up around my ankles.

"Stop fussing!"

"Well, start talking."

I turn away from her and face the window. There's a squirrel staring in. He's holding half a walnut and freezes like he's been caught stealing. I watch him put it in his teeth and scamper away. I stay quiet and slow my breathing so Mom thinks I'm sleeping. Finally I feel the bed shift when she gets up and leaves.

I'm just starting to doze off for real when the door slides open again.

"Come on, get up now. We're going out to the porch."

"No, Mema, it's too cold."

She drags the wheelchair up next to the bed and locks it in place. "You're a tough girl. You can handle it."

No, I'm not tough. I'm an invalid. In-valid. I want to say it, but I know she won't listen. There are certain statements Mema refuses to hear.

Ten minutes later we are out on the porch wrapped in a blanket and holding hot chocolate that is already only luke-warm. The garden looks shriveled and sad, like it'll never grow another living thing again.

"All right, your mama's in there walking a hole in my carpet because you won't talk to her. Now, it has been a million years and a lifetime ago since I was in middle school, but I remember the feel of it. Those days stick to you like mud. Talking about it is the only way you're gonna come clean again."

I look into my mug. She says she gets it, but Mema is a force of nature. I'm not strong like that. How am I supposed to make her understand?

"I promise, Ellie. You talk to me and I'll take as much of it away as I can and we'll leave it behind us. You hear me?"

I look at her. Her small, round eyes are as blue as the early morning. She pulls me in so my head's up against her shoulder and her braid hangs down between us. I want to tug on it like I used to when I was little. Talking's not going to make it better, though. I want a time machine. But I tell her anyway.

Eight hours earlier . . .

Coralee's next to me in the van. We actually see the bus stop at the entrance to Royal Oaks right as we turn off Alcoa onto the main road, and I make Mom wait until it's out of sight before we pick up Bert. The last thing we need is to be the handicapped van that tails the bus to school.

Bert's sitting on his front steps. His trailer is bigger than ours and Coralee's put together, and it has a porch that wraps all the way around. I guess this is the rich end of the road. He gets up and, I kid you not, throws a man purse over his shoulder.

"Nice purse," Coralee says when we make him get in the front seat.

"It's a satchel, as you can see from the flap by which it closes. Purses traditionally have a zip or clasp. Morning, Ms. Cowan."

He would have been right at home on the short bus. We kept to ourselves and did our thing and just assumed from day one that we were all up there on the weirdness scale. But here, oh man. What does a place like Eufaula do with a Bert? Or, more to the point, what does a Bert do with a place like this?

"Bert's parents just moved into Royal Oaks in the fall, same time as me," Coralee says, leaning forward so the glitter from the heart on her sweatshirt

134

sparkles. "Right, Bert?"

"That is correct." If it's not a purse, he sure hugs it like one.

"Bert has twelve brothers and sisters. The twins just graduated high school last year."

"Lucky number thirteen," I say.

"Thirteen is conventionally unlucky," he says, and that's the end of the small talk.

As Mom is lowering me down from the lift next to the front doors of the school (she doesn't even try for the handicapped spots), she says, "Now, they don't have an official aide for you yet, but Rachel in the front office will do until Mrs. Rutherford can find someone permanent."

"*Mom,* I don't need an aide." I whisper it because Coralee is waiting for me with her backpack slung over her arm, which *is* a purse in leopard print. Bert has already wandered off.

"Ellie, you had an aide back home. Lauren helped you get from class to class and in the restroom only when you needed her. I've instructed Rachel to do the same."

"But I don't get as tired now. I'm stronger than I was. Please don't make some old lady follow me around!"

Mom is zipping my lunch into my backpack and ignoring me. "Rachel isn't some old lady, honey. She's Evelyn's niece."

"You have got to be kidding."

"I am not." She hangs my backpack on the back of my chair. "And you will be fine, because you're right, you're stronger than you were, inside and out," she says, and kisses me.

"All right, all right, stop with the mushy. I'm going," I grumble.

None of the other kids look our way, but they shift so me and Coralee are a bubble of aloneness in the crowd.

I look back once, even though I wasn't going to, right before we move through the doors. Mom's still there, cupping her hands together like she's praying.

Coralee is in A group, so she has a different homeroom. I end up having to say good-bye to her halfway down the hall. She blows me a kiss and straightens my backpack like Mom did.

"Be good, honey-baby-child," she sings, and walks away backward, right as Rachel puts a hand on my wheel. Her face is powdered so white she looks like a ghost, except for the peach lipstick, which is also on her teeth. I remember Evelyn at church. It must be genetic.

"Ready for your big first day?" She is not a big person and she's not standing too close or anything, but something about her makes me want to shrink down in my chair like a turtle. She smells like that really strong perfume at the department store — the one they're always spraying in the air and trying to give away in free samples.

"Thanks. I got it from here."

"Okay, Lily. Now, if you need me, I'll be in the front office. And if you need to use the *bathroom,*" she whispers, "just get a pass from your teacher and come find me."

Never, never, never, I think as I roll into homeroom.

Homeroom with Mrs. Tilly is crowded. I mentally graph the room and immediately see that the desks are too close together for me to fit through. They are in four rows of five, and bookshelves fill up every single wall.

I start to breathe a little fast and clamp my mouth shut so nobody can tell.

Mrs. Tilly isn't here yet, but almost every student is. And everyone freezes. I'm wearing jeans and a green sweater, the most basic thing I could find, but suddenly I feel naked.

I don't know what to do. Normally, I use my wheelchair with my tray on it as my desk, and the teachers leave a blank spot open for me in with all the other desks.

I wheel forward toward the front, near the teacher's desk, and try to scoot along the far wall. There are backpacks in the way. Everybody pretends not to notice and nobody moves them. So I try to roll back around by the door, but one wheel gets caught on the edge of a rug in the area with a sign that says READING NOOK.

I want to cry.

I will not cry.

Now I'm sweating. Where is the teacher?

People start moving again, getting out books, sending last texts (probably about me), but nobody helps.

I'm reversing out the door when I hear it.

"Ellie! Back here." Bert is waving from the last row. And then he's standing and kicking backpacks out of the way like soccer balls, while three girls in front of him shout, "Don't touch my stuff!"

Once the path is clear, I follow him back with my head down. The bell rings, and Mrs. Tilly walks in ten seconds late in a wave of flowy skirts and scarves. She is, unsurprisingly, also my English teacher.

"Sorry! Sorry! Late, late, late. New Year's resolution already broken. Well, there's always next year. Ha, ha!" She pauses, take a big swig of coffee, and then holds her hands out. "Lily! I see you've made it! You go by Ellie, right?" The girls in front of Bert laugh into their hands. "Let's see if we can't do a little rearranging, shall we?"

And then she makes everybody stand

up and push all their desks five inches to the right, which basically does nothing. It is screechingly loud and I want to disappear. But that's the one thing you can't do in a wheelchair.

Next to me, Bert is sharpening an old-fashioned number two pencil and is completely unaware of everything else going on in the room. For one second I wish I could be like him. And then, because Mrs. Tilly was late and homeroom is only ten minutes, the bell rings and I have to leave to do it all over again.

And it happens in every class.

There are exactly twenty desks and every room takes rearranging and all the teachers are nice and none of them look like they have ever had to do this before. My science teacher, Mr. Miller, yells, "Can you hear okay in the back?" like my CP has also made me deaf. My speech teacher, Mrs. Roman, takes five minutes to tell the class about her cousin who also has cerebral palsy and is now working as the manager of a Target in Edmond "in spite of it."

I don't drink any liquids all morning so that I don't have to use the bathroom, but by lunchtime I am dying, and luckily the whole sixth grade eats together, so Coralee comes with me and guards the door. I hear her growl at someone from outside the stall.

It's only eleven thirty, and all I want to do is go home, but we head into the cafeteria instead.

Mom has packed me a peanut-butter-and-honey sandwich and a squeeze pouch of applesauce. One of my leftover linzers is in there too, but it's so hard and dry I can't even bite all the way through. The tables in the lunchroom are in long rows with stools attached (of course), so I have to sit at the end. Coralee sits to my right, and I don't even mind when Bert takes the other side. Without saying hello, he unwraps a chicken salad sandwich with a Food & Co. sticker on it. I bet everything he eats comes straight from the day-old deli counter.

"So I already have homework in history, math, and Spanish," Coralee says, and takes a bite of her pizza. She's the only one that bought hot lunch. "How? I mean, how is that possible?"

"It costs the government eight thousand dollars a year to send one student to school. Of course the teachers are going to give you homework. It would be financially irresponsible for them not to."

"Bert, we need to work on your filter," she says.

I want to talk. But I'm just so tired. I unscrew the applesauce.

"You all right over here?" It's Rachel. She crouches down next to my chair with her hand on my arm. And that's all it takes — one adult to make all forty kids in the room look my way.

I see someone from homeroom, one of the girls, the blond one that wouldn't move her backpack. She looks at my squeeze pouch and laughs. I push it under the table.

"She's fine." Coralee shoos Rachel away and she leaves, but her perfume hangs around and puts me off my food entirely.

I shove my entire lunch back into the bag. I wish I could crawl in too. How do I explain that those squeeze pouches were the only fruits and vegetables I could eat for a long time? "Easy calories," Mom says. I can't help it that I still like them. I must look like such a baby.

Coralee grabs my lunch and starts setting it back out again.

"They're not laughing at your lunch. It's just the trailer park thing."

"What trailer park thing?" Bert asks. It's the first time he's looked up since he sat down.

"There's us" — Coralee points at our table — "and there's them," and she waves her arms around the whole room. "The trailer park kids and the townies."

"That's not a thing."

"It is, *Robert.* You've just never noticed because you're a bit off. No offense."

"A bit off what? The average?" He looks at us both and folds his sandwich wrapper into a square. "If so, I'll take it as a compliment."

"So what's the trailer park thing?" I say, turning so I won't have to see the blond girl. I still can't pick up the squeeze pouch.

"Now listen, you two. I've lived a lot of

places with my mama, see." Coralee points her crust at both of us. "And there's always a line. A railroad track, a street name, a bridge. Doesn't matter what it is. But there's always some place that separates the weird from the normal, the poor from the rich, the white trash from the middle class."

"But my mom's a teacher and Bert's dad runs Food & Co." I don't say anything about Dane and Susie because I'm not sure what they do, exactly.

"It doesn't matter. It doesn't matter if we brick down the sides and plant little gardens, or what kind of cars we ride around in. A trailer's still a trailer, even without the wheels."

I let that sit a minute.

"So everybody's staring at me not because I'm in a wheelchair. It's because I'm from the park?"

"You got it, sister. You're from Trailer-land now."

The only redeemable part of the entire day is gym, and that just proves how bad it was overall.

For a brief and terrifying moment, Rachel tries to help me change in the locker room. But Coralee chases her away again, and after a hurried emergency meeting between Principal Rutherford and Mr. Hutchinson, they decide to let me stay in my jeans. I just have to change into the yellow shirt with the lion on it.

Unlike in every other class, Mr. Hutchinson has a plan for me from the moment I wheel onto the waxed floors. All the girls have gym together, and we are separate from the boys, thank Jesus. So there we are in a circle in the center of the basketball court, and Mr. Hutchinson starts to take everybody through stretches. Before I can even start to get embarrassed, though, he hands me two long, stretchy green bands.

"Triceps first, Cowan," he says. And this is something I can totally do. I've been using these for arm and leg stretches for years. They look like giant rubber bands. I do triceps and biceps, and then when everybody gets up to run laps, he helps me loop the bands around the bottoms of my feet and pull up to stretch my calves. It feels good. I've been slack about my exercises since we moved. I'm supposed to stretch every day to keep everything loose. I can feel all the tightness where it's built up in my ankles.

"Where'd you learn to do this, Mr. Hutchinson?" I ask him while he switches out the green bands for purple ones that are stretchier.

"Call me Hutch. You mean how does a gym teacher like me know how to do real therapy?"

"No, I just mean . . ." I fumble with an answer, because yeah, that's exactly what I mean, but when you put it like that, it just sounds rude.

He laughs and rubs the back of his head. "Just teasing you, Cowan. I trained as a physical therapist and worked with the athletic department at OU before coming here."

Before I can ask why in the world he would leave a college position for this, he stands and blows the whistle for break. Half the girls pull out their phones, which they are not supposed to have in class, but Hutch doesn't notice or just doesn't care.

"I'm glad you're here, Cowan. It lets

me practice my skills. Now rest up, because this next part you can do with everybody else."

And then he blows the whistle for everybody to run the lines. They have to run back and forth from wall to wall, and I race along in my chair with everybody else, pumping my arms as hard as I can until I feel like my lungs are on fire. I feel like one of the extras in *Murderball,* that movie about the Paralympics. I always wished I had a chair as cool as theirs with the huge wheels that tilt in. Coralee jumps on my lap for the last round, and I just about drop her at the free-throw line.

If gym had been the last class of the day, it all might have been fine. I mean, still terrible, but bearable. But then I have Spanish, and then we have dismissal, and dismissal is worse than all the rest put together.

After the final bell everybody, fifth through eighth grade, files out at the same time and waits in the same long line between ropes like at an amusement park. Except instead of a ride, you're waiting for your bus. Different buses pull up to different spots, but you can't get on your bus until it's your turn in line.

To be clear, this is a terrible organizational idea.

But none of this should have mattered, because me and Coralee and Bert were riding in the van. Except car kids aren't allowed to cross to their vehicles until all the buses are gone. And Rachel, being Rachel, decides she has to stand with us until my mother or other guardian "is visible." And so I sit hunched over in the cold while *every single student* files past me.

If they had stared or even laughed, it would have been better, because then Coralee could have said, "What are *you* looking at?" and Bert could have cited the temperature at which water becomes gas or something like that, and we'd at least have had something to do. But nobody even looks at us. It's like we aren't even there. And I spend the entire time wishing I weren't, because it feels like I don't exist. Even Coralee doesn't look up from her shoes until all the buses have driven off in a cloud of fumes and we all hear Mom calling and waving from, yes, one of the handicapped spots not ten feet away.

"So how was everybody's first day?" Mom asks when we finally pull out into traffic. But nobody says a thing — all of us silent and staring out three different windows.

"Well, that's not *so* bad," Mema says. I give Mema one of my best Mom eyebrows. "I mean, that Rachel's a pill, and two thirds of your teachers sound like space cadets, but none of this is unfixable."

The hot chocolate's long gone and my fingers are frozen. Mema hugs me tight. We're sitting in the glow of yellow from the kitchen window now that night has set in.

"I can't do it all over again."

I didn't cry all day, but now I do a little. Just the idea of going to sleep only to get up and have to go back there makes me so worn out, I can't even move to get myself back in my chair.

"But you don't have to, honey."

She takes my face in her hands, and somehow they're still warm.

"You will never *ever* have to have a first day again. You've already done lived that. Firsts are the worst, that's what I say. First dates, first kisses, first days, first jobs. Now it's on to day two, and who knows what's waiting for you?"

She means it to sound exciting, but it just sounds scary. Who knows what's waiting? I didn't tell her about all the stuff Coralee said about the trailer park. I don't want her to think I'm ashamed of where we live. I love this place. I always have. It's okra and blackberries in the summer and fishing at No. 9 landing and shelling beans on the porch. I wouldn't trade it for anything.

"Okay." I start unwrapping us from the blanket. "But Rachel has *got* to go." I say it loud and sassy, because Mema wants me to be brave, and maybe if I pretend to be, it'll turn true.

"Oh yes, honey, that girl might be worse than her aunt, and that's saying something."

"Mom will never go for it — me not having an aide."

"You let me handle your mother, sweetheart. What's the good of being old as dirt if you can't pull rank?"

8
CHALLAH AND BASKETBALL

Dear Deb Perelman at smittenkitchen
.com,

I have been thinking about God
lately and what it means to "live a life
according to your convictions," as my
grandma's pastor would say.

I've never been good at the prayer
thing. I mean, I pray sometimes, but
only when something really, really
bad is happening or I think might be
about to happen. I don't think that's
the same thing as just praying because
you'd like to tell God about your day
or you're just so happy or whatever.

The thing is, I've been pretty worried lately and so has my whole family, and so I've been trying to get back
to talking to God about all that stuff

because maybe it might help somehow.

And now I know you're wondering why I would write to you about all this when you are a famous cook and this is about a Jewish recipe and my grandparents are Methodist and I'm not even sure what my mom and I are.

But I have a reason. It's this: I came across your challah bread on your blog, and you say even the smell of it could "make a religious person out of you," and I like that. I like the idea that baking can be another way of talking to God. So maybe when I bake, it counts as praying and God understands where I'm coming from.

Anyway, all that to say . . . thank you for this wonderful challah recipe, which my grandpa insists on calling "cha-la" instead of "hol-la." Everybody loved it, and it made our little kitchen smell as good and sweet as you promised. And you are right — it was even better the next day as French toast.

A grateful fan,
Ellie Cowan

I'm making more challah on Sunday afternoon after church and a lunch of salmon patties and green beans. The kitchen is covered in flour and so am I, but it's warm in here and the windows are all fogged up and it's nice, like I'm snuggled in a sleeping bag. I need something to take my mind off school, and punching dough and braiding it like hair is exactly the thing to do it.

I wish I could make bread instead of pie for the contest in May. Bread is trickier — like the final exam of baking. It would kick a lot of people out of the running.

Wheeling myself all over school, plus doing the laps in gym, has made my arms feel like jelly, but I'm not telling Mom because, miracle of miracles, she actually gave in and is letting me go without an aide. Rachel still waves from the office and tries to come over, but I shoot off before her perfume gets me.

At lunch on Friday, Coralee tried to explain the sixth-grade groups to me, but she called them "tribes," and at first I thought she meant Native American tribes. We are in Oklahoma, after all. But when I said, totally innocent, "Like Cherokee and Sioux?" she spit her Coke out onto the table and laughed until Bert told her that you could rupture your spleen that way.

"No, Ellie darlin'." She gets more Southern when she thinks she understands something you don't. "I mean gangs. The kids who run together."

She pointed at the end of our own row of tables, where a group of six boys sat with their heads together over a piece of paper. "Those are the basketball players. They're probably talking 'strategy' for the game tonight," she said, using our favorite air quotes. I could see their long legs sticking out at all angles from under the table. Yep. Definitely basketball players.

"Who are they?" I asked, and nodded toward the three girls in the row next to us. It was the blond one and her friends from my homeroom who had laughed on that first day. They always wear shirts with words on them like "luv" and "l8r" and short, short skirts with UGG boots. It makes me cold just to look at them.

"Ick. Yes. Those are student government girls."

"Wait, seriously?" I said, because they did not look like the type to care about hall passes and the price of Cheetos in the vending machine.

"Seriously. They only do it so they can plan the dances." Coralee leaned over and pointed a french fry in their direction, and it was so obvious that I grabbed her hand and pulled it down. "What? They're too busy pretending not to watch the basketball guys to notice. That's Sierra in the middle. She's on the beauty pageant circuit. She'll be at the one in Checotah I'm going to in March."

"Wait. You're doing a beauty pageant?" I couldn't make my voice normal, and Coralee noticed, because then she was pointing at me.

"Yes, I am *doing a beauty pageant,* and don't judge. How else am I going to get noticed? In case you didn't know, I'm not lined up to be on *The Voice* anytime soon. Besides, my talent is singing and you know I will kick every girl's tail." She took a bite of her bologna sandwich and talked through it. "I am going to be the next Kacey Musgraves. So you better be nice to me."

I snorted and stole one of her fries. I thought beauty pageants were for five-year-olds with crazy moms.

"Who are they?" Bert asked, and I was glad because it made Coralee stop giving me the stink eye. I turned to where he was pointing just as obviously as Coralee. These two clearly hadn't spent a lifetime trying to blend in. I think that fact, more than the trailer thing, might have been the reason we were the only ones at that table.

The table Bert pointed at was the only one besides ours where guys and girls sat together.

"I'm surprised you don't know," Coralee says. "Those are your kind of people, Bertie. Those are the *mathletes.* They're the smarties, and they travel together doing math competitions and probably play chess in each other's townhomes on the weekends."

"I don't like math," Bert said, doing his slow-blinking thing. "I just like facts."

I'm coming to learn that Bert isn't creepy weird like I thought. He's just a mega geek. If he lived back in Nashville, he'd probably have his own tribe of geeks

157

just like him to calculate statistics and memorize all the former presidents of Lithuania. But in Eufaula he's just about the only one. We had all these cliques back at home too, but our middle school was four hundred people.

Now, in Mema's kitchen, I think about how easy it was to get lost in the crowd back home as I pull the challah, warm and golden, out of the oven.

Grandpa wanders in first. He taps his knuckles on the countertop. "Mmm-hmm, something is calling my name."

I slice us both a piece and top it with a little butter and honey. I hand him his wrapped in a paper towel, and he eats it leaning against the counter. He looks a lot younger today in his jeans and cowboy boots. Maybe he's just more rested. I haven't heard him up and about in the middle of the night in a while. And the bruise on his nose is mostly gone now.

Mema has told me more than once how they met. He was nineteen and she was fifteen, and he rode up to her on a horse. Like, he literally *rode up to her* on a black stallion and said, "Would you do me the honor of a date?"

And it worked.

He did rodeos back then, and she says he looked like "God or the devil" when he rode up to her dressed all in black from head to toe with his red hair shining.

He took her to a fine "eye-talian" dinner, as he would say. I bet they split spaghetti like in *Lady and the Tramp.* They got married when she turned eighteen, and that was that.

I watch him now as he closes his eyes and chews slowly.

"Baby girl, this might be the best thing you have ever made. We're gonna have to hide this from the women, or there'll be none left by suppertime."

He winks and wanders out again. It's stuff like this that makes me glad we're here, even if Mom has to drive me to school and carry me into the bath and the squirrels will not shut up at six o'clock in the morning.

"You *are* coming to this game whether you want to or not."

"I can't think of anything I'd rather do

less than watch a bunch of dudes run up and down the court while I sit in my chair at the end of the stands like a grandma."

I am lying on Coralee's frilly white daybed and trying to stretch my toes. It's something Hutch has got me doing to help with the aches that keep me up at night. He might be the best PT I've ever had, but I'm not telling Mom or she'll stop feeling sorry for me. Then I'd have to wave good-bye to the extra ten minutes' sleep in the morning and half hour of screen time at night.

"Nope." Coralee throws a stuffed unicorn at me. "You do *not* get to pull the cripple card. I am singing the national anthem in front of God and the entire middle school, and I want my best friend there to witness."

That catches me off guard. I've never had a best friend. Ever. The closest I came was in kindergarten when a girl named Pammy decided we would be friends and pushed my chair around on the playground at recess. This is way better. I want to hit pause on life for just a minute and savor it, like the most perfect first bite of pie. But Coralee's aiming a pillow at me, so I say, "Okay, I'll come! But I'm bringing Bert. With all his brothers and sisters gone, I think he's lonely."

"Robots don't get lonely."

"Don't be like that."

"Like what?"

"Like a townie."

"Aw, I was just kidding. You know I love that weirdo."

The next night I'm sandwiched between Mom and Bert in a crowd of people trying to file past concessions. I keep an eye out for elbows. I actually got a black eye once when we were waiting in line to see Santa at the mall.

It's already one thousand degrees in the gym, and even though middle school sports are like Mommy and Me playtime compared to high school, there's still a pretty good turnout. I spot Sierra and her clones in the front row taking selfies. Coralee's nowhere to be found.

"She'll be warming up, no doubt," Bert says, sounding suddenly British, which is what happens when he gets nervous. He's got on a Lakeview Lions sweatshirt, but there's a collared oxford underneath. And instead of sneakers, he's wearing loafers with actual pennies in the tops. I guess I should give him points for trying, at least.

"You two want anything from concessions? Soda? A Snickers?" I know Mom's asking only because she's looking for an excuse to get something herself. We hardly ever keep candy in the house.

"PayDay, if they have it," Bert says.

"Reese's for me, please. Bert, you *would* like an old people's candy bar," I tell him. "Come on, let's get to the front. Coralee made me promise to take pictures."

I let him steer me because it's just that crowded, and we get right up next to the rail of the stands. I spot Hutch squatting in front of the team in their folding chairs on the sidelines. He sees me and waves just as Mom gets back. I didn't know he was the basketball coach, too.

"So that's your gym teacher whom I spoke to on the phone," Mom says, and hands me a Sprite and my Reese's. It's already soft from the heat.

"Yeah, Hutch, Mr. Hutchinson."

I watch her size him up like Mema does a melon that might possibly be rotten. And then the lights flash and both teams stand and Coralee walks out like a queen to the middle of the court. Her hair is bigger than I've ever seen it, like LEGO hair, and she's wearing a red, white, and blue skirted leotard. Under the court lights, she sparkles like a firework.

She takes the microphone from the ref like a pro and leans toward the home fans as if she's about to tell them a secret.

"Evening." Pause. "Y'all ready to salute our fine country?" Pause. "And then beat those Badgers into submission!"

Everybody goes crazy — yelling and clapping and whistling, or booing from the visitors' stands. The ref shakes his head. But Coralee just winks at everybody and turns to face the flag.

She takes two deep breaths like she's about to dive, and then starts.

"Oooo-uhhhh say can yoooouu seeeeeeee . . ."

It is low and strong and beautiful and I am only just realizing I have never heard her sing for real. Normally, she's just humming in the van or singing half lines in her room.

When she hits "O'er the ramparts we waaaaaaaatched," it's like she is another girl altogether, and I have no trouble believing she'll be famous. It's so powerful it shakes my heartbeat all up. Even Mom has her mouth open in a big, silent O.

I forget to take my phone out for pictures until the end, when Bert grabs it and starts framing shots. When it's over and the applause dies down, she turns back to the crowd, takes a bow, and then says real low, "Coralee out," and drops the mic. I whistle with two fingers like Mom taught me. Hutch laughs and bends over to pick up the mic and hand it to the ref. Back on the stands, Sierra is pursing her lips like she's sucking on a Gobstopper. I hope singing isn't her talent for the beauty pageant. Actually, I kind of hope it is.

"That was amazing, Coralee honey!" Mom says when Coralee runs over to us with a towel slung across her shoulders. She's breathing like she just ran the mile in gym.

"Thanks, Ms. Cowan," she says, and then turns to me. "Did you get pictures?" Bert hands over my phone. That's the last I see of it for the rest of the night. She plants a big smacking kiss on his cheek that turns him bright red, and I laugh into my sleeve.

None of us watch the game, and the Lions lose by ten, but the night was a success. I don't even mind that not a single person spoke to me outside of Mom, Coralee, and Bert. Three is enough. Three is more than I've ever had before.

9
CUPID'S ARROW

Mom is sitting on the floor in the living room with papers spread around her like a fan. It's another Friday night, and Mema and Grandpa have gone to church for a potluck. I'm at the dining room table staring at one single blank sheet of paper. I have to give a speech on Monday, and according to Mrs. Roman, it has to be a demonstration speech where I teach the class something. Other than wheelies in the chair and how to whistle with two fingers, I'm out of ideas.

"You want tea?" I yell over my shoulder.

"Yes, please." And then after a minute, "But, honey, you don't have to scream. This house isn't big enough for that."

I bring us two mugs of chamomile and the Thin Mints from Mema's Girl Scout cookie stash in the freezer.

"So, what are you doing?" I say, leaning over the papers. At first I think they're essays she's grading, because she's been subbing a lot for the teacher who just had a baby. But I didn't think they let subs grade papers.

"Careful there!"

She wipes crumbs off the top sheet and then starts to turn it over, but I catch a few words at the top and grab it. "Autumn Leaves Assisted Living." My throat closes up.

"What is this?"

She sets down her tea and sweeps her hand over the whole pile, gathering it up like a stack of cards.

"This, Ellie, is just in case. I've been talking with Dr. Hirschman and trying to come up with a plan for what to do when we can't take care of Grandpa anymore."

"No." I roll back and hot tea from my mug sloshes over on my legs. "That's why we're here, Mom. To take care of him so he doesn't *have* to go anywhere else. *You* heard Mema. We are family. This is what we do."

Mom's the fixer. But putting Grandpa

in a home isn't a fix — it's giving up. She's breaking all the rules. I've never wanted to get up and run out of the room more in my life.

"Ellie, listen. I know we're family. But I also know what happens when you leave it too long. It's not good for anyone." She rubs at her forehead. "You think I *want* to put my father anywhere?"

She's acting like she's trying to talk it through with me, but she's not really. She's talking *at* me. She thinks because I'm twelve, I won't understand.

"So that's it, then? He does a few things that inconvenience people and we ship him off?" I tip my chair back, like a horse rearing up, and then let it thump down hard. It's the closest thing I can do to a stomp and it's not nearly good enough.

She doesn't answer.

I feel the tears start, and the words come before I can stop them. "Is that what you'll do to me, then, if I get to be too much for you to handle? Do you have a file of 'homes' for me, too?" There. I've said it. The thing I've never even let myself wonder until now, because Mom would never do that. Except I never thought she'd put Grandpa in a home, and here we are.

I'm crying and I hate it and I see her looking at me like *she* wants to cry or hug me, and I can't handle that, either.

"No, Ellie! Oh, never!"

I don't want to hear it. I know she'd never really do it, but I feel dizzy, like the air's been sucked out of the room, and I want to lay my head against something cool, a windowpane, a glass of ice water, until everything stops spinning. I roll away and down the hall so I can be alone in the dark.

Everybody says what they want you to hear until they change their minds. I thought we had an unspoken code, Mom and me. When Dad left, when the seizures were so bad, when I hardly had a friend at school, when we came here — no matter what happened, we had each other. Because family is family. But I guess not. I guess family is only family as long as it's convenient. I mean, I know what's going on with Grandpa is not like what's going on with me. I'm not getting sicker. I'm not a danger to myself or other people. It's different. But it *feels* the same.

There was a girl, Rita, at my elementary school, who I never told Mom about. She was in my grade but was already two or three years older. She had CP and some other stuff too — she drooled and wore a bib and couldn't talk much. But she seemed to understand what was going on. She would follow us with her eyes on the playground from her motorized wheelchair in the shade.

They bussed her in every day from the children's home. That's what it was . . . a children's home for disabled kids whose parents couldn't take care of them. I don't know if they just gave up or maybe they were old or poor or had too many other kids to look after. Whatever it was, Rita ended up in the home. They always dressed her bad — mom jeans and old Disney sweatshirts, so she looked like a giant toddler. And even though I know they probably did their best to keep her clean, she always smelled funny — like hospital sheets and diapers.

She was at school for only a couple of months. And then one day she was just gone, off the roster, and nobody told us what happened.

One look at Autumn Leaves and all I can think of is Rita.

Saturday is glitteringly bright with the sun shining off the ice on the grass. Mom didn't say a word to me last night when she finally came to bed.

I woke up in the middle of the night needing to go to the bathroom but stayed awake and held it until my stomach cramped. I wasn't about to ask her for help. I tried praying to keep my mind off it. I prayed for Grandpa to be healed and for Mom to settle down and for Coralee to win the beauty pageant and for me to get strong enough to walk better so I won't need help from anybody ever. I hoped God or Jesus or whoever was listening.

Now I'm mixing up a batch of snowball cookies after lunch because I don't want to talk to anybody or work on my speech. I'm just licking the spoon, wondering if I could make a piecrust out of this almondy sweetness for the contest in May, when someone knocks on the front door.

"Well, who do we have here?" Grandpa

says, and steps back from the door.

I lean back from the kitchen to look down the hallway. You can see just about every room in this place if you lean back a little. For a minute I don't recognize him. His dark hair's slicked back and he's in a suit so white it hurts my eyes. He's holding a giant bouquet of red roses that match his bow tie.

I roll down the hall slowly, like I'm on my way to the principal's office. When I get up close, I see a sticker for Food & Co. on the green plastic wrap around the flowers. And then he kind of throws them at me and I have to catch them in my lap, which sends a dust of powdered sugar from my hands in his general direction.

"Bert," I say, like I'm talking to a tiger that's gotten loose from the zoo, "what are you doing?" And then I calculate back in my mind to that first visit to school and those posters I have seen on the bulletin boards ever since, and it clicks. It's the second weekend in February.

"No. Uh-uh." I brush the flowers off my lap and onto the floor, and then I back out of the doorway. "I am *not* going

172

to the Valentine's dance."

Bert opens his mouth. I hold up my hand like a crossing guard.

"No," I say. "Do you know how many bad movies there are where the poor little crippled girl goes to the dance? No way. I am *not* sitting in a corner while everybody drinks Hawaiian Punch and takes selfies and tries to dance like Beyoncé."

I can see it in my head — me, sitting at the edge of some sad strobe light while everyone around me pretends not to see. I look at Bert in his too-white suit and too-big shoes. Wallflowers unite. No thank you.

Mom and Mema join Grandpa at the door behind me. Bert bends down and picks up the flowers, totally calm.

"Well, hon," Mema says, "why don't you let the boy get a word in edgewise?"

I point a finger at her. "You're in on this, aren't you?"

Mema winks and Grandpa looks at his shoes. Mom is currently the only one who looks as confused as me.

"Who said anything about the dance?" Bert says, and I'm spinning around between people, trying to figure out if this is one big joke.

"We're not going to the dance?"

"Nope," Coralee says, stepping up beside Bert and scaring the daylights out of me. She came from behind the holly tree again wearing her red dress from Christmas Eve. But now she's covered in glitter and has a headband with heart-shaped antennae on her head. She looks like a very shimmery ladybug.

"Do you think for one second I would go to a *middle school* dance? Laaaaame," she says.

"So where are we going, then?"

"It's a surprise."

"Then I still say no."

Bert holds up his hand like a Boy Scout. "I promise, where we are going, you will not have to dance." And then he places the flowers gently on my lap.

"Promise on your most favorite purse."

"It's a satchel."

"Promise on your most favorite satchel."

"I promise."

"All right, all right."

"Rock on!" Coralee yells. "You have exactly half an hour until this ship sails!"

Mema turns to Mom and smiles. "You don't mind, do you, Alice? I told Bert's dad you'd drive."

Mom and Coralee follow me into the bedroom. I stare into the closet like it will magic the perfect outfit out of thin air. But how do you pick what to wear when you don't know where you're going?

"Warm or cold?"

"Definitely jacket weather," Coralee says, and sits down at Mema's old sewing machine in the corner. I stare some more. Corduroys. Sweaters. Jeans. T-shirts. Two winter dresses and three summer ones. Behind me I hear the pump, pump, whir of the sewing machine. Coralee's got her foot to the pedal, and the empty needle bobs up and down.

"Do I have to wear a dress?"

"Do I look like your mother?"

"No. No, you do not."

Mom pipes in. "Honey, I'm not sure

about this. It is twenty-five degrees out." She puts a hand to the window. "Why don't your friends stay here? You all can watch a movie." We haven't said more than two words since I found her with those papers for Grandpa last night.

"I'm going. Where are my red leggings?"

"Oh, I've got just the perfect thing to go with those!" Coralee jumps up and runs down the hallway.

I hear the door open and slam shut. I can't hear anything else. I wonder what Bert's doing in there with Mema and Grandpa. Probably reciting the state capitals or mapping the stars or something.

Mom turns from the window, and her hand leaves a foggy outline like a ghost. "You need more than leggings. Where's your long underwear?"

"I am not wearing long underwear!"

"Ellie, I do not want you to catch a cold."

I yank on my leggings but can't get them all the way up. It's easier on the bed, but I don't want to take the time to get myself out of my chair.

"I am not a baby," I say, which would have been much more impressive if she hadn't been pulling my leggings up over my bottom.

"I know that."

"I don't think you do."

I hear the door open and shut and Coralee's feet pounding down the hallway.

"Got 'em!" She's holding her white sweatshirt with the glitter heart and a red feather boa.

The best thing about Mom driving is that I can pretend she's not here. Bert's up front giving directions because he won't tell even her where we're going, which proves he is much cooler than people give him credit for. It's midafternoon now but still sunshiny, and I close my eyes for just a minute because it's warm in here. Next to me, Coralee is humming something about the Chattahoochee River, and already this is better than any old dance.

Half an hour later we pull into a parking lot. It's totally empty. There's a white fence running around the block with a tiny building about the size of Mema's canning shed in front, and that's it. I can't see what's behind the fence.

"We'll take it from here, Ms. Cowan." Bert holds his hand out to shake hers, but she ignores him. She's squinting at the building as we all unload. I say "building," but now that I'm closer, I think technically it's what you would call a shack, like the kind they serve snow cones from at the beach. The walls are big sheets of plywood nailed together and painted white like the fence. There's a counter, but it's taller than I can see over. Bert runs around the back and pops up behind the counter like a puppet. He unrolls a canvas sign and it falls down the front.

I read in bright blue letters: BILL AND WILL'S PUTT-PUTT EMPORIUM.

"Ta-da!" Coralee says, and twirls in a circle. "Miniature golf is the perfect anti–Valentine's Day activity, right?!"

Mom shakes her head.

"Ladies," Bert says, and passes down golf clubs.

"Bill and Will?" I say.

"My twin brothers. They built the place."

"Your parents named your brothers Bill and Will?"

He shrugs. "They didn't know they were having twins. They only picked out one name."

We choose our ball colors out of a bucket. I'm purple. Coralee's red. Bert is blue.

While we wait for Bert to unlock the gate, Mom leans over me and taps my jacket where I've got my phone. Her breath makes a cloud. "I'll be here if you need me. You call me when you're done or if you get too cold."

I nod, but when she tries to stuff mittens in my pocket, I roll away. Everybody knows you can't play miniature golf with mittens.

The gate creaks open and Bert waves us inside with his club over his shoulder.

"Let's *do* this!" Coralee yells, and races through.

It's a proper eighteen-hole course and

it's kind of amazing. It's got a Western theme. There are holes that look like saloons and deserts and a train filled with gold. There's even one with a horse's tail that swishes back and forth in front of the hole when you turn on the switch.

"I can't believe your brothers did all this."

"They're on scholarship for engineering," he says, like of course it's totally normal to build a full-size miniature golf course in your spare time. I'm beginning to think Bert is the most normal one in his family.

"Me first!" Coralee yells.

"Hold on. Hold on." Bert pulls a tiny scorecard and pencil out of his white jacket pocket. He looks like the guy on the front of the popcorn box. Or Colonel Sanders. "We have to make it official."

"Whatever," Coralee says, and drops her ball.

I smile. They have no idea.

Coralee hits like she's trying to make it to the moon. Her ball flies off the rocks and back down the green. One time she has to chase it into the parking lot. Bert is worse. He's so precise, it takes him five minutes to line up a shot. But he almost always gets it in the hole in two or three swings.

By the fifth hole they both stand back and watch when I roll up to tee off

What I did not tell them when we pulled up is that I have been playing miniature golf since I was three. Mom and I went to the fun park out near the mall all the time in the summer. While the other kids ran off to the go-karts and the bumper cars and the arcade, I stayed with Mom on the greens.

And so now, after nine years of practice, I can line up, lean over, hit the ball one-handed . . . and get a hole in one almost every time.

Mini golf is my jam.

"You're like a golf goddess," Coralee says when I hit one over the water and through the Grand Canyon to the hole on the other side. My hands are freezing and I can't really feel the club, but I nod.

"Yes. Yes I am."

It's getting darker now, and I think of the other kids heading off to the dance and feel sorry for them.

"Did you know that seven men died in the Saint Valentine's Day Massacre in 1929?"

"Bert, jeez! Filter, remember? You're up, anyway," Coralee says.

He lines up his shot for three minutes and then finally swings, but misses the hole that is just to the left of a wooden cactus. It's only by half an inch. But a miss is a miss. He takes out his scorecard, makes a note, and then walks forward. He's still talking when he steps up and taps his ball in. "Well, did you know that Saint Valentine was a priest who was martyred and buried on February four-teenth in a city near Rome?"

"Bert." I poke him in the shoulder with my club.

"My point is, you two, that miniature golf is a much more appropriate pastime for Valentine's Day than a dance or date or dinner. Romance has no place on this holiday."

"Except dinner sounds good now." I wipe my nose on my sleeve.

"Okay," Coralee says, "this is the last

hole. Then dinner."

But I grab both their clubs before she can take her running start. Even though I'm pretty sure my toes are blue inside my boots, I still want a minute to take a mental picture of all of us head-to-toe in red and white like candy canes on the eighteenth hole. My club is across my lap, and I can hear the water from the hose running through the canyon. It's perfect. It's the best Valentine's Day, or any day, really, I've ever had.

"What?" Coralee says.

"Nothing, just sizing up my victory shot."

"Nah, don't you know the rules? Who-ever gets a hole in one on the last hole is the *real* winner."

She takes a flying leap, and we all duck when her ball shoots off the bucket of gold on the little wooden train and comes flying back at us. Bert catches it with surprising reflexes.

I, of course, take the hole in one.

■ ■ ■ ■

We stop at the Dairy Queen on the way home and pick up burgers and chocolate-dipped cones. It's so cold, even in the van with the heater running, I have time to eat my entire burger before the cone starts to melt.

It's completely dark when we roll down the gravel drive after dropping off Bert and Coralee. Mom and I sit in the car for a minute. I'm so tired, I close my eyes.

"Did you have fun, sweetheart?"

"Yeah, I did."

"And you're glad we're here?"

"I'm glad we're here."

"And school's better? At least better than it was? The teachers are giving you enough time between classes and you're all right without an aide?"

"Yeah, Mom. Things are better."

Better but still not great, I don't say. People still don't really look at me or talk to me, other than adults and Bert and Coralee. But then again, nobody really talks to anyone but their own friend group anyway.

"Good, good. I just want to know you're taken care of," she says, reaching her arm back and rubbing my knee. "And I'm sorry about last night. I'm sorry you had to find out that way. Grandpa's not going anywhere for a long, long time. I promise, okay?"

"Okay. Can we go in now?"

I want to believe her. I do. But I can't get that picture of the Autumn Leaves brochure out of my head. This is the first time all night I really feel the cold.

I spend all of Sunday, the day before my speech, blowing my nose. But I don't mind because miniature golf finally gave me an idea.

10

SPEECHES AND AMBULANCES

Speech class with Mrs. Roman is fourth period, right before lunch, which makes my topic just about perfect. But when the bell rings at the end of third, all I want to do is throw up and hide.

I have to get Bert to carry all my supplies. We make sure to get there early to stash everything up by the whiteboard. There's one speech before mine. Keith demonstrates how to dribble between his legs. But he never looks up at the class, and his ball hits his foot and knocks Mrs. Roman's trash can over. Everybody still claps and whistles, though, because he's on the basketball team.

While Keith is cleaning up the trash, I remind myself: *Make eye contact, pause, enunciate, ask for questions.* This is the first time I'm going to have to talk to the entire class *and* they will have to talk back. Class participation is part of their grade too. I cough into my elbow when Keith sits down and say a quick prayer. Then I roll forward as Mrs. Roman calls my name.

I've never baked in front of anyone before or had to narrate it like I'm on a cooking show. It's weird, like I'm one of those kids with their own YouTube channel.

With Bert as my assistant, I take the class step by step through the cookie recipe I was making on Saturday. It was the miniature golf that gave me the idea. Bill and Will made something amazing because it was something they loved. They didn't care if anybody else liked it or thought it was strange. So I decided to do the same thing — I would do something I'm good at, even if nobody else cared.

I set out the flour and butter and bowls. Nobody says anything. But technically, I guess they aren't supposed to yet. When Bert drops the cookie sheet, it sounds like a thunderclap and everybody jumps. But it finally gets me talking.

I begin to explain the history of the snowball cookie, "otherwise known as a Mexican wedding cookie or Russian tea cake," I say.

Keith starts to text under his desk, and only about a third of the class is even watching what I'm doing. But then, once I begin to scoop out the dough and roll it in the powdered sugar, people start to lean forward to try to see in the bowl.

Sierra raises her hand. I mean, she actually *raises her hand* to ask a question and not to fix her hair or pass a note. At first I don't know what to do. You're not supposed to take questions until the end, but then I nod to her because my hands are busy, and she says, "What's that ice cream scoopy thing?"

"This?" I hold up the metal scoop I'm using to portion the dough. "This is actually a melon baller that I found in my grandma's kitchen drawer. But they make real cookie scoops, and I'm going to get one once I become a professional baker."

I can't believe I just said that out loud, but Sierra just says, "Cool."

"Yeah. Cool."

When the cookies are laid out on the

baking sheets, I explain about preheating the oven and cooking time. Then, because I am aiming for a big finish, I pull out the Tupperware filled with the snowballs I made yesterday and pass it around. Everybody cheers and Sierra takes two, because as I said, we are only minutes away from lunch and the whole class is starving.

I get more claps than Keith. All that's left when the container gets back to me is a little pile of powdered sugar.

Dear Editors and Bakers at Southern Living,

I found your recipe for Almond Snowballs in my grandma's 1989 holiday baking issue. I liked the picture, and it seemed like just the thing to make when you're tired of real snow but still stuck in winter.

It was also for a grade in class. It went well. At least, I think it did, because I didn't have any left afterward and everybody clapped. Luckily, I didn't actually have to bake them in front of everybody, because that would have taken fifteen minutes of us staring at one another with nothing to do, and also, we don't have an oven in class. I brought in my most perfect batch. But man, are they messy! I think all the powdered sugar stressed out my teacher, but she still ate three.

So, thank you for helping me to get a good grade and for thinking up a recipe from so many years before I was born that people still like. I get why people want them at their weddings.

Many thanks and wishes for warm weather your way,

Ellie Cowan

"Ellie was amazing," Bert says at lunch after my speech.

"Ugh, I wish I could have been there. I tried to get Susie to write me a pass, but she said I had to take my history test or I couldn't go to the pageant." Coralee shoves her spoon around her banana pudding. She only gets it for the Nilla wafers. "I like her and all, but sometimes I wish it were just me and Dane and the cockatoos."

I tear my sandwich into little pieces and then roll them into balls. It's hot in the cafeteria, and the two snowballs I ate in class are making me feel funny. I wish I'd bought a water instead of Coke. But I'm so happy that my speech is over and that it went well that I don't even care.

"You guys, they looked at me and it wasn't just to laugh or check out my chair."

"Who?" Coralee asked.

"*Everybody.* The townies, Mrs. Roman, the whole class." I spread my arms wide.

"Like I said." Bert nods. "She was amazing."

"Well, don't get used to it," Coralee says, pointing her spoon at me.

"What?" I let my arms fall on the table.

Coralee looks over to where Sierra and her friends are trading bags of chips. "I said — don't get used to it." And then she looks at me. "A townie's a townie for life."

My stomach swirls and gurgles and I press into it with my fist.

"And what about us?" I say, punching

at my lunch bag like bread dough. "Are we trailer kids for life?"

"Honestly?" She looks from me to Bert. "Yes. We are."

I wait for her to say she's kidding, but she doesn't.

Bert stares at his hands.

"Why are you being like this?" I hate it that my voice has gone all high, but I can't help it.

"Like what?"

"Mean. And like you can't even let me be happy for one second." I feel the beginning of tears but blink hard. I am *not* going to cry at the lunch table. "Why can't you let me just be normal?"

There's a pause that feels like a million years, and then Coralee taps my chair.

"Ellie, honey. You'll never be normal."

And then I do start to cry.

So I back away.

Roll fast down the hall.

Turn the corner into the gym.

And throw up all over the court.

■ ■ ■ ■

It's too bright in this room. I can feel it before I even open my eyes. And something's over my face, trying to smother me. It's too tight. I can't breathe. I tug at it, but my hands are heavy and I can't get it off.

"Honey, honey. Relax, baby girl!"

I open my eyes. Mom's over me. She's taking my hands and pulling them away, but she's not getting the thing off my face. I pull at her and push, but she won't let go.

Her head moves in front of the light, and now everything's in shadow.

"Where?" But I can't talk because the thing is covering my mouth, too, and my fingers aren't working right. My chest hurts.

"Rest, honey. Just rest. We need you to —" but I'm already falling asleep.

It's night now and there's something cold in my nose. It shoots air like icicles down my throat, and I yank it away. Something beeps over my head, and then alarms go off, like ten alarms all louder than the loudest setting on my phone.

A nurse runs in with Mom behind her and puts the little tubes back into my nose and then gently hooks them behind my ears. She's wearing Doc McStuffins scrubs.

"Honey, you've got to leave this in. I know it's itchy and cold, but it'll help you breathe," she says.

I start to cry. Everything hurts. My legs are tight, and it feels like something's sitting on my chest.

Mom leans past the nurse and hugs me, and that makes it hurt worse. I yelp, and she jumps back and starts crying.

"Oh, not you, too." The nurse turns to Mom. "Let's get you something to eat. I'll stay with Miss Lily here until you come back."

Mom shakes her head. She's grabbing on to the bed rail like they're going to have to drag her out.

"Now, Mom, we need you to keep your strength up so you can take care of your girl," the nurse says. "We're all trying to get her out of here as soon as possible, but it's not going to be tonight, so you might as well make your way down to the cafeteria."

The nurse's arms wobble over my head as she pushes some buttons on the monitor.

Mom doesn't move. The nurse pats her hand, the one still holding the rail.

"I'll have them bring you up a tray, all right?"

Mom nods.

I fall back asleep.

It's day again, but I'm not sure what day. The tube's gone from my nose and they've propped me up a bit. Mom is asleep in a chair next to the window. Her hair's flat on one side and straight up on the other. She used to have hair as long as Mema's. I remember when she first cut it off. I was six and in the hospital after this one seizure they couldn't stop. I just kept shaking and shaking. Once I was a little better, Dad came to visit and Mom left for a while. When she came back, all her hair was gone, up above her ears and everything. She looked like an elf.

She hears me moving and jumps up. The blanket wrapped around her falls in a puddle on the floor.

"Ellie, you're up!"

I try to rub my eyes, but there's an IV in my hand and it pinches to move it.

"You'll be able to get that out as soon as you finish the last of your antibiotics." She points to the baggie of liquid hanging near my head. "They say if your oxygen levels stay stable, we'll be able to leave in a few days."

"Seizure?" It feels like I'm talking around rocks. Please, God, don't let it have been a seizure. Don't let me have to go back on those meds, with everyone treating me like I'm a bomb about to go off any second. Please don't let the count start again, X many days since the last episode. Please.

She hands me a big pink jug with a bendy straw and makes me take a sip of water before she says anything. I forgot about the ice, like little pellets of sleet. Hospitals always have the best ice.

"You got an infection, baby. It turned into pneumonia."

Well, that explains it, the feeling like a horse was stamping on my chest. I've had pneumonia before, but it's been a few years since I was in the hospital for it. I'd take it over being the "seizure kid" again, any day. But Mom doesn't look like she'd agree.

"How long have I been here?"

She rubs my arm above the IV.

"Four days."

"Four days!"

"They had to keep you pretty sedated for most of it. You kept trying to pull off your oxygen mask."

"But I've got school! I missed my history test!" I try to sit up farther now, but the pillow slips and I can't find the button on the side of the bed.

"Ellie, we will figure all that out later. For now, you rest. Look. They brought a few DVDs up from the lending library."

I flip through them. *Frozen. Hannah Montana. The Muppet Christmas Carol.* I am six again.

■ ■ ■ ■

A few days later and there's a knock on the open door. Mema and Grandpa walk in with a dozen giant balloons shaped like cupcakes. They float up to the ceiling and bob along in the breeze from the air vent.

"There's my girl!" Mema says, and leans over to hug me, and thankfully it doesn't hurt.

"Hi, Mema. Hi, Grandpa."

"Ellie, love, you gave us quite a scare," Grandpa says.

They're in their church clothes, and Grandpa's got a bit of tissue stuck to his chin from cutting himself shaving. He smells like Dial soap and leather. I start to cry.

I'm just so tired of all of this, and I don't mean the hospital. The wheelchair thing I can handle. But I hate it when the rest of me doesn't work. That's what nobody gets — the CP isn't only about not being able to move my body; it also makes my whole system weak. I get sick more than most people. I get worn out more than most people. I get ambulance rides and hospital stays for stupid reasons. And I hate it.

"Okay, you two, why don't you go down and get me some coffee. Ellie and I need another minute," Mom says, and they shuffle out the door.

I wipe my eyes on the blanket.

"Ellie." I look up. Mom's in advocate mode and I don't like it. "We need to talk."

"What about?"

"We need to talk about our situation."

"What situation?"

"I spoke with your father."

The word "father" lands at my feet like a rock through a window.

"Why?"

"He's concerned. Wait — let me finish. I am too. Honey, this place just isn't as equipped to meet your needs."

"No." I wave my hands at her even though it hurts with the IV. "No. We're *not* going back. And since when is Dad concerned about anything having to do with me?"

"Ellie —"

"No!" I hit the call button on the bed.

Not two seconds later a doctor comes in with a clipboard.

"Ms. Cowan. Lily. Here are your discharge instructions. We're sending you home on oral antibiotics, but remember, you've also got a follow-up appointment in one week here at the hospital."

She sets everything on the counter by the little metal sink and my pink water jug.

"If you'll just sign here? And I'll have a nurse come in and get that IV out for you, and you'll be good to go."

I look over at Mom — her mouth is still open with all her unsaid argument behind it, but she moves to sign, and I've bought myself just a little more time.

11
Pageants and Court Cases

Spring snuck in while I was sleeping. Daffodils and crocuses shoot up underneath the empty trees. I can see green, too, on some of the bushes outside the bedroom window.

I don't think I realized just how terrible it is not to be able to move. I mean, I *know*. Of course I know. But at least with my chair, I can *get* around if not *move* around, if you know what I mean.

I've been sitting in this bed and staring at the wood panels running up the walls for five days now. It's almost March and outside the sun is showing off. But I'm stuck in here listening to the squirrels and watching reruns of *Cupcake Wars* on my iPad. I can't practice for the Bake-Off. I can't do much of anything. But I did get Bert to text me homework, and

I'm already caught up. Mom sees me doing it and doesn't say anything. She hasn't brought up going home again, but that doesn't mean she's changed her mind. Mom never changes her mind.

Unluckily for her, I don't either.

I turn onto my side and grab the stretchy bands Hutch brought over yesterday. Apparently, he's the one who found me in the gym and called the ambulance, which is so humiliating — that image of me slumped over in the chair, probably with puke on my chin. I wrap a green band under my foot and pull. All those days in the hospital ate away what little muscle I had. I look down at my legs, skinnier than ever, like scraggly tree branches, and pull harder.

My phone buzzes.

ellie stop ignoring me

im sorry

i didn't mean it

ur my best friend

ok fine

im txting until u txt back

txt

txt

txt

And then she sends every emoji in the list.

I turn off my phone. I haven't talked to Coralee since that day in the cafeteria. It's not that I'm mad. Okay, I am mad, but she's also right.

I'm *not* normal.

I had eight days in the hospital and a million hours in this bed to think about it. I'm never going to be like everybody else. I'm never going to run the mile in gym. I'm never going to walk without the gait trainer. I can't even reach the fountain drinks at McDonald's.

But I don't need Coralee to remind me.

Dear Dad,

Thank you for the flowers and the card. Mom says you've been worried about me, so I'm writing to tell you I'm fine. You don't need to fly out here. I promise I'm better.

I'm still stuck in bed, though, so the iPad's come in handy. So thank you again for that, too.

It sucks because I haven't been able to bake since I've been home, but Mom promises a few more days and I can get back to it. I guess I've never told you that I like to bake.

Maybe next time I see you, I'll make my oatmeal raisin cookies. Mom says those used to be your favorite. I kind of like them too.

Ellie

"Knock, knock."

"Hi, Mema."

"I brought you one of my sudoku books. Thought you might be bored of staring at the wall and giving your mama the silent treatment."

She hands me *Jumbo Sudoku* and a sharpened pencil. She's got on her gardening shoes and smells like turned-up earth.

"I'm not giving her the silent treatment."

"Oh, all right. The teenage treatment, then. One syllable at a time."

"She can't make me go home."

"Oh, honey." She pulls my hair back

and starts to braid it in a fishtail like she used to when I was little. It feels good.

"Your mama just wants to do right by you."

"Don't I get a vote?"

"Of course you do, love. But we've got to keep you healthy, and maybe this isn't the place to do that."

"So you're kicking me out?"

I pull away from her hands and look at her.

"What? No. I would never kick a member of my family out. Unless they criticized my cooking, and you would never do such a thing."

"God wouldn't want you to give up on me." It's a sneaky move, throwing God at her.

She's not fooled. "Don't you throw the Good Book at me, Lily Belle Cowan. God *knows* I am not giving up on you. And you do too."

She lets my hair go and stands.

"You and your mama need to talk. Woman to woman. Work this out." She picks up the pink jug that the hospital let me take home. "I'm putting sweet tea in this thing, see if it can't sweeten you up."

After a week at home, Mom and Mema finally let me off bed rest. They help get me back in my wheelchair, and I take a slow tour of the trailer. It is sweet freedom to roll down these halls and into the kitchen.

My arms are shaking by the time I get there, but I let the kitchen fill me with its yellow glow. It feels like the first time I've breathed since the pneumonia.

I'm digging in the fridge for lemons when Mom walks in and leans against the counter.

"What are you making?"

"Lemon poppy seed scones."

"Sounds delicious."

"I wanted something springy, and lemon is Grandpa's favorite."

"I think they'll be a hit, but you might want to tell him they're biscuits. I don't think he's heard the word 'scone' in his life."

"Thanks for the info." I shut the fridge

hard and the lemons roll off my lap.

Mom sighs and picks them up.

"Ellie, we need to talk."

"Then talk." I know I'm being rude, but I don't care.

I start sifting the flour and sugar together.

"You're not going to look at me?"

"I've got work to do." I'm making up a lemon custard in my head — thinking about that for the Bake-Off, thinking about anything but this conversation. May feels so close and I need to focus.

"We came here to help out with your grandpa, because that's what families do. But, Ellie" — she stops my hand from mixing, takes the bowl, and kneels down in front of me — "you have to understand something. *You* are my first priority. I have never been so scared in my life as I was when they called me from the ambulance. You weren't *conscious,* honey. You were barely breathing. I can't lose you, Ellie. I can't."

Now she's crying into my lap like a little kid, which makes me start too, because everything makes me cry these days. I wipe my nose on the dish towel and hand it to her, and she does the same. Something cracks in me and I know I can't win this. Nobody fights fair when it's family.

"What about Grandpa?"

"We'll come back in the summer. See how things are. The's no rush to make any decisions about his care yet."

I nod into her shoulder.

"It's not forever. It's just for now."

She leans back and we both just sit.

"If I might interrupt this Hallmark moment," Mema says, coming in from the living room, "you have a visitor."

Coralee walks in wearing a puffy gold ball gown. She has to turn sideways to get through the door.

"Let's take this out on the porch," Coralee says after Mom and Mema leave.

"Take *what* out on the porch?"

"This. This thing between you and me. It's sixty degrees and sunny, and your grandmama already said if we're going to yell, we have to take it outside." She puts her hands on her hips like something out of *Gone with the Wind.*

"I'm not going to yell."

"Fine. It'll just be me, then."

"What do *you* have to yell about?"

"Come outside and I'll tell you."

Out on the porch the sky is bluer than it's been all winter, and when the breeze shifts, I get the smell of wild onions. Mema's been digging in the garden.

Coralee takes a seat on the rocking couch and her skirts fly up like a Hula-Hoop.

"Lookit, we just drove in from the pageant," she says, and I can't believe I forgot that was today, but she doesn't give me even a minute to feel bad about it. "And I had a bit of a light bulb moment when I was onstage, and I've come to tell you about it."

"Are you wearing fake eyelashes?"

"Ellie, hush, and yes, and let me get this out."

I wait.

"I know this might make you madder at me, or maybe you can't get any madder than you already are. Either way, I'm going to say it anyway." She takes a big breath like she's about to sing the anthem again — "Ellie Cowan, you are not normal."

"Thanks. Can I go in now?"

"No, let me say my bit. Ellie, you are not normal, *but* I wouldn't want you to be for all the tea in China. And I would have *told* you that if you hadn't stormed off, or if you had answered any of my texts."

She's plucking at the torn seam in the couch and not looking at me. Not a single hair on her head moves in the breeze. It's got that much hair spray in it.

"I know that," I say at last.

"You do?"

"Of course I do. But you listen to me" — I poke a finger into her hoop skirt so she'll look at me — "Bert's not the only one who needs to work on his filter."

"I know. I know. And I'm sorry you got sick."

"Yeah, me too." I know I should tell her now that Mom is shipping us home. Instead I say, "So did you win?"

"Nah, second. But Sierra didn't even place, so I consider it a victory."

"Why aren't you dancing a victory dance, then?"

"Well, the thing is . . ." Coralee pauses for a moment, and for the first time I realize she looks a little sad, wilted around the edges despite the huge hair. "I thought my mama might come today. She said she would when she phoned last week, so I figured there was a fifty-fifty chance. But then the landlord from our old apartment called Dane today. Said she'd skipped out on the rent, disappeared."

Disappeared. We let the word hang there like a deflated balloon. I want Coralee to look at me, but she's picking at the couch cushion like it's her job. I've never had a close enough friend to feel like I let them down, until now. I should have remembered the pageant. I wish I could reverse time and be there, so when she looked up in the crowd and didn't see her mom, she'd at least have seen me.

"Do you know where she went?"

"Nah. She'll turn up, though. She always does." The way Coralee says it, all low and slow like Eeyore, I can't tell if that's a good thing or a bad thing. Then she finally looks at me, and I have never seen her so serious in her life.

"Listen, Ellie, that's why I had to come over." She puts a hand on my chair. "I don't have a lot of people. Dane, Susie, Bert, and you. That's it. And none of us is what you'd call 'normal.' But you're my family."

Something inside me flips over like a pancake, and I know I can't leave her.

I'm about to stir up a whole world of trouble. But I can't help myself. I put a hand on Coralee's satiny shoulder and say, "My mom's moving us back to Nashville. And you've got to help me stop her."

The plan is simple and comes together over a three-way call between me, Bert, and Coralee. The next afternoon I'm out on the porch shelling peas with Mema when they both come around the corner and march up the steps. Bert's got his dad's laptop under his arm.

"Afternoon, Mrs. Cowan. We're looking for Ellie's mom," Coralee says. Today she's wearing a pin-striped skirt and suit jacket, and her hair's slicked back in a bun. Bert is right behind her in a suit and tie. They look like lawyers.

Mema takes one look at them and winks. "I'll just see if I can't find her, then."

When Mom finally comes out and Bert leads her to the rocking couch, she eyes him like he's a Jehovah's Witness.

"Would you like some water, Ms. Cowan?" He's brought his own and offers her a bottle.

"No, thank you. I'm just fine, Robert. Ellie, what's this all about?"

I put on my best poker face.

"I've got no idea, Mom."

I can see Mema and Grandpa watching through the kitchen window. Mema slides it up slow and easy, so they can hear when Bert clears his throat.

"Ms. Cowan. It has been brought to our attention by a source that would like to go unnamed" — I can feel Mom's eyes slide toward me — "that you plan to take Ellie home to Nashville. And while we understand your concerns, we would like to ask for the chance to state our case."

He pauses, and we all wait for Mom to react, but she stays quiet. I let out a little breath I didn't know I was holding.

Bert hands Coralee the laptop, and she clicks it open to the PowerPoint we spent all of last night on.

"We know Ellie's pneumonia took a lot out of both of you, and you worry about her care while she remains here in Eufaula."

He nudges Coralee and she clicks the first slide.

"But if you will take a look at the chart, you will see that the weather here averages eight percent less humidity than in Tennessee."

Coralee clicks to the next slide and another chart pops up — this one a map of the Southeast next to a map of the Southwest. Bert pulls a laser pointer out of his pocket and points first to Tennessee, then to Oklahoma.

"And because of the slightly later blooming season, our allergens tend to be a good deal tamer than in your typical Southeastern region."

Mom puts a hand up. "Wait. You two know I love you, but this is not about humidity and allergies. This is about Ellie's safety."

"Mom, hear them out."

"No, Ellie. The closest children's hospital is in Tulsa. Did you know that? And what about school? They don't have a proper aide for you. You can't even ride the bus, for heaven's sake!"

"Mom, the school's fine! Riding in the van is fine! And I don't need an aide!"

I practiced this. Practiced it without yelling, but I can't stop now. "You don't understand! I *have* to stay. Home was so . . . lonely." It's a weak ending, but it's true.

A second passes while we stare at each other, and another passes while she swallows and blinks like she's got something in her eye.

"But you will always have me, honey?" Mom says, like it's a question, and I take a breath and then answer it.

"I know, Mom." How do you tell your own mom she's not enough? Or she is, but you want more than just enough?

Luckily, I don't have to, because our ringer comes whistling around the corner.

"Hutch! Mr. Hutchinson!" I say, and wave like this is just *such* a crazy coincidence.

"Jim! What are you doing here?" Mom stands up and tugs at the sides of her shirt.

"Alice."

Apparently, sometime between the ambulance and now, Mom and Hutch got to be on a first-name basis.

He takes the porch steps two at a time. Thankfully, he's changed out of his tracksuit and into jeans and a button-down. Bert offers him the bottle of water, and he accepts with a smile.

"Alice, I've had the chance to get to know your daughter pretty well over the last few months. She's a determined girl, and I've seen what she can achieve when she pushes herself. She's more motivated than half my students in gym."

"But pushing herself too hard is what got her sick in the first place." Mom's looking back and forth between all of us like she can't tell where to aim her argument.

"I understand that, Alice, but I think I can help if you let me continue working with her. I can show her a few more exercises, gentle ones, that can build up her strength."

"Mom, he's the best PT I've ever had."

"Three more months," Coralee pleads. "That's all we want. Just let her finish out the semester before you decide."

"Come on, darlin', you know when you're outnumbered," Grandpa shouts through the window.

Mom walks to the edge of the porch. She stands there with her back to us.

After a minute when nobody moves, she says, "Lord help me."

It's all I need to hear.

"Wahoo!" Coralee yells, and spins.

Mema says, "That a girl!" and Grandpa slaps the table.

Hutch just walks down the steps, nods at all of us, and says, "I'll see you Monday, Ellie."

"Don't look so disappointed," I say to

Bert, who's standing there with his hands in his pockets.

"Yeah, what's eating you?" Coralee says.

He closes the laptop slowly and picks it up. "I had twenty-eight more slides."

12
TEST KITCHEN

The first few weeks after I came back to school, everybody was really nice to me. Like, *really* nice to me. All the teachers talked to me like they talk to the soccer players when they come back from concussions.

"Ellie, you just take it easy now. You get tired, you tell me."

"Ellie, Nurse Patsy has been made aware of your special circumstances. You go lie down anytime you need to."

"If you need extra time to get to class, Ellie, you just let me know."

It was super annoying.

The only teacher that didn't do it was Hutch. He even made me wear ankle weights to try leg lifts. He's printed out all the exercises and made a binder I have to work through. I've never had homework in gym before.

The students were weird in the beginning too.

My first day back Sierra texted me at lunch: u want to eat w us?

I looked up and she waved, and I half waved back. It was nice and all, but I couldn't imagine going alone, and Coralee would probably set their table on fire, so I just said, nah im good. thx though, and waved again and she was fine with it.

Later, in speech, she asked me for the recipe for the snowballs, and I wrote it down on the back of her English notes.

Everybody's mostly back to normal now that a month's gone by and I haven't collapsed in a puddle in the middle of the hallway. One good change stuck, though. People stopped looking *over* me and look *at* me now. It's nice. Easy. I guess getting sick and disappearing for a while finally turned me visible. Or maybe it was the snowballs. Food is the universal hello.

Now I'm in the kitchen and I'm practicing. I realized something while I was making the cookies in front of the class: I'm my best self when I'm baking. I'm patient and I'm not nervous and I'm good at it. And so now I'm trying to be great at it.

The fish fry is coming up soon, and the big pie Bake-Off. I thought I'd have more time to prepare, practice my skills, but being sick sucked all the time away. And now this is the final part in the plan that I didn't tell even Coralee or Bert. This is the final piece that will prove to Mom that we have to stay, past the summer, into seventh grade . . . maybe forever. It will prove I am more myself here and happier here than I could ever be in Tennessee.

No pressure.

For years I've had to listen to Mema tell me over the phone about the chocolate mousse or the cranberry apple or the double butter pecan that's won. The winner gets a one-hundred-dollar gift certificate to Food & Co. and a big blue ribbon. It's always some mama or grandmama who's been baking her whole life, and it's a recipe that's been passed down for twenty-five million generations.

It's always a safe bet that wins.

But not this year.

This year I am going to be the youngest baker in history to win, and it's going to be with something brand-spanking-new.

Except I have no idea what to make.

The counter is covered in cookbooks. Some are Mema's and the pages stick together. Some are mine I brought from home — ones that used to be Mom's that she never used. I've also got every single cooking app open on my iPad. Still nothing.

Grandpa walks in and side-shuffles toward me with a whistle. He's been in the garage doing his woodworking, and he smells like sawdust and oil.

"You could catch flies with that mouth, baby girl. What are you thinking so hard about?"

"I want to make something amazing for the pie contest." I point to the books. "But everything's already been made."

He walks over to the counter and flips a couple of pages. I see a bruise on his arm as big as a quarter. It's plum purple and I wonder how he got it.

"Well, as the Good Book says, there ain't nothing new under the sun. Seems to me like you've got to pick what speaks most to you."

I think on that for a minute. He's right, of course. The problem is, nothing's talking at the moment.

"Think of it this way," he says, and drinks down a cold glass of water from the sink. "If you were a pie, what pie would you be?"

I haven't got the first idea. He sees my face and laughs and pats my shoulder on his way back out.

"Don't worry about it, Alice baby. You'll figure it out."

He hasn't called me Alice in weeks.

13
BERT'S TINY TOWN

It's damp and dark, but I don't reach out to pull the cord dangling from the light bulb. Nobody knows where I am. I wasn't even sure my wheelchair would fit down the ramp.

But it did, so I'm sitting in the quiet in the pitch black of the canning shed. I don't need the light to know that rows and rows of mason jars sit on the shelves higher than I can reach. Mema's set mousetraps everywhere, so I don't hold out a hand. But I know what's here. Beans and okra and tomatoes and peaches and blackberries and strawberries and apples and squash. Everything from the garden, waiting to be brought out into the light.

Somewhere in here something's got to speak to me.

Or not.

Because after twenty minutes in here, I still don't know what in the world to do, so I back on out when I hear Mom calling and move on to plan B or C or W or whatever I'm on now. I get her to drive me over to Bert's.

We pull up, and I feel a little hesitant for a minute. I've never actually been inside his house. It's beautiful, baby blue all around and white porches, like it could be on the cover of *Better Homes and Gardens*. If *Better Homes and Gardens* ever featured a trailer.

There's no ramp, though, no way to get to the front or back door, so Mom has to go up and knock for me. Mrs. Akers steps out and gives Mom a big hug. I know Bert's dad from years of shopping at Food & Co., but I haven't met his mom before. She doesn't look anything like I pictured, like Mrs. Claus or Mother Goose or whatever you look like after having thirteen kids. She's tiny, with a neat gray bob, and she's shouldering a satchel that looks a lot like Bert's. I forgot she does all the accounting for Food & Co. I guess Bert gets his smarts from all sides. I can't hear what they're saying, but Mom nods and smiles and walks back to me as Mrs. Akers gets in her car and drives off.

"Bert's out back, honey. Want me to push you?"

"Nah, I got it."

I roll across the grass toward the backyard before she can ask me why I needed an emergency visit to Bert's. I didn't tell her I was actually hoping to catch Mr. Akers.

But when I come around the corner and into the yard, there's nobody there at all. Just a few apple trees and a patch of weedy garden near a shed. I look back, but Mom has already disappeared down the drive.

"Hello!" I yell, and a couple of birds shoot off from their spot on the telephone wire.

The door to the shed creaks open and Bert's head pops out. His hair is crazier than usual — like a Chia Pet.

"Ellie."

"Bert."

He looks embarrassed, like I caught

him stealing or smoking or watching anything on the CW.

"Uh, I was actually looking for your dad. I wanted to ask him a few questions about some spices he might have in the store. But, uh, I can come back."

"No. Stay." He walks down the little ramp from the shed but then just stands there. I forget sometimes that without Coralee around, Bert can be hard to talk to.

I rock a little in my chair. Some of the blossoms from the cherry trees land on my shoulder. Bert reaches down to pick them off, and I see he's got something in his hand.

"What is that?"

He pulls it back and looks down, like he forgot it was there. We both look together. It's a tree. A tiny tree carved out of clay, no bigger than a dime.

"This is a blackjack oak, native to the Southwest, particularly here in Eufaula."

He holds it up an inch from my nose.

I look closer. It really does look just like the trees all over town.

He cups it and points to the shed.

"Well, you're here now, so I might as well show you."

He helps me up the ramp to the shed, and I see it's bigger and brighter in here than I thought. There are windows at the back that let the light spill across the floor, or what would be the floor, if it weren't covered in a teeny-tiny town. It's like looking down from an airplane window.

"This is Eufaula," Bert says. He half smiles but won't look at me.

I lean down to get a better look. There's the lake in the middle and an actual metal bridge that connects our side to the rest of town. I spot the church and our school, and back down by my feet is Bert's blue house and also mine and Coralee's. He even made a gravel path. The Dairy Queen up the road has an actual sign that lights up. Red Oklahoma dirt runs underneath it all.

"Bert. This . . ." I can't find the words.

"I know, it's frivolous, really. Just a bit of fun." Uh-oh. He's gone British. He rushes forward to block my view.

"No, that's not . . . It's beautiful." It's

not the right word. Maybe genius? Or epic? But it makes Bert calm down a little. "Move out of my way. I want to see it better."

He steps aside and points out the grocery and the Dollar General and the tiny cars crossing the bridge. I spot the Putt-Putt Emporium and something clicks.

"You helped Bill and Will design the course, didn't you?"

He shrugs.

"Why are you hiding this? It's amazing!"

I take the tree from his hand and study the leaves. Apparently, it's autumn here. The leaves are all reds and yellows. He sighs and points to the corner, by the window. For the first time I notice the damage. The hills are smashed and cracked, like they were hit by an earthquake. Houses are toppled into the cracks.

"Some guys at school found out."

"What do you mean 'found out'?"

"I stayed after history one day to ask Mr. Rollins if he had any old printouts of the town, and we got to talking about it. I guess word got out."

He won't look at me. I turn back to the damage. It's like a cake sunken in the middle and crumbled to bits.

"Who did it?"

"I'm not sure. But there were notes in my locker. 'Dudes don't make doll-houses, Roberta.' Stuff like that. They smashed up a lot more of it, but I've been able to repair a good chunk so far."

"Didn't you try to find out?!"

Bert flinches. I didn't mean to yell, but *come on*! I'm furious.

"Look, Ellie, I don't want a fight. I just — I just want to be left alone." He takes his tree back and sets it in a patch of light near the lake. I reverse back out into the yard. I want to hit something.

"It happened just before Christmas. It's why I stopped riding the bus."

Oh.

"Like I said, I'm working on fixing it. Dad ordered me new plaster, and the new blackjacks just came in to paint."

"Can I help?" It's the least I can do if I

can't punch somebody.

"You want to?"

"Sure."

And so for the next two hours, we sit in the sun and I paint trees in greens and golds. The breeze is cool and we don't talk. For a little while I forget about anything else but the tiny leaves. It's like baking — a totally mesmerizing act of creation.

14
A REVELATION

I wake up with waxed paper stuck to my cheek. I fell asleep at the kitchen table last night after testing a gazillion recipes. It's less than a week until the fish fry, and I've still got no clue what I'm going to do. And now I'm waking up to one less day, and the birds are tweeting outside like this is a Disney movie.

I had that dream again, the one where I can walk.

I wake up in my bed at home, but home is back in my pink room in Nashville. And instead of reaching out for my wheelchair like I always do, I sit up and swing my legs over the side of the bed instead. Just like that, I am up.

Mom is yelling from the living room to "get a move on it" or we'll be late, and so I run down the hall into the bathroom. And this is the beauty of it all: I take a shower. I stand under the water and let it fall all down me and swirl around my toes. I look down and my legs are strong, like with actual muscles, and my kneecaps don't stick out like knots on a tree. I start singing some Carrie Underwood song, which is proof this is a dream because, hello, country music is not my thing.

And then when I come out, Mom is in the kitchen sipping coffee by the stove, and her hair is long again, and when I go to hug her, I can look right in her eyes because I am almost as tall. I am almost as tall.

I hate that dream. Because most times the wheelchair just mildly sucks. But after those nights it sucks big-time.

Mom walks in while I'm peeling the waxed paper off my face.

"There you are! I can't believe you slept in here."

"Yeah."

She takes in the jars of canned goods, the half stick of butter, the empty carton of eggs, the baking soda spilled down the side of the microwave.

"Did you figure it out?"

"Well," I say, rubbing the crusties out of my eyes, "it's not custard or caramel or almond or strawberry or chocolate or licorice."

"Licorice?"

"I'm ruling nothing out."

"I'm not sure process of elimination is your best bet here, El."

Mom sweeps a big pile of eggshells into the trash under the sink.

"If you have a better idea, you let me know."

"Hey, don't get sassy with me now. You want me to help you with a bath?"

"No." The dream is still too real. "I'm going to lie down for a little bit."

"All right. We've got church at ten, though, and you know your Mema."

In church, I try a different strategy.

Dear God,
   Please help me find the perfect pie, the one that's the most me. Or at least give me a hint.

234

And also, I know you saw that dream last night, because according to Genesis, you know just about everything. I want you to know that I'm not going to ask for that, okay? I'm not going to ask for some sort of miracle.

But if I were going to ask for a miracle, would you please help Grandpa? I don't mind the CP so much most of the time, but I think the stuff with Grandpa is driving him a little crazy. Or crazier. And I don't mean that in a mean way. I mean, I think he's tired of being confused, and I think maybe that might be worse than not walking? So I guess I'm asking, could you please make him better?

And also help me with my pie.

Amen.

I don't know if it was the prayer or what, but when we bow our heads for the benediction — the blessing at the end of the service — I get an idea.

■ ■ ■ ■

"You want me to rinse these for you?"

It's the day of the fish fry, and I've just put the pie in the oven. If this one isn't perfect, there won't be any time for a re-do. Coralee is sitting on the kitchen table, smack on top with her legs crossed like she's about to meditate.

"No. Stay where you are. This kitchen is tiny enough as it is, and I need the space." It's also a thousand degrees in here, so I lean over her and open the window.

"You think 'Yellow Rose of Texas' is a bad thing to sing in Oklahoma?" Coralee's been practicing for a new pageant in July.

I shrug. Four months in the state isn't long enough to give me an opinion.

"Oh well, I don't care. I love me some Willie Nelson," she says, and then hops down. "I'm off to get changed. See you for your victory lap." She's still humming when she passes Mema on her way out the door.

"Well, this place has never smelled so

good in my life. What you got in there, a slice of heaven?" Mema tries to peek into the oven, but I block her.

"No. Uh-uh. You've got to wait for the big reveal like everybody else."

"All right, all right, Miss Thing. But as soon as that's out of the oven, you've got to get yourself down to the bedroom. Your mama sent me to tell you it's time to shower and change."

I stop to look at Mema. She's like summer come early with her white capris and red-and-white checked shirt.

"You look like a picnic table."

"Well, thanks a lot." She fans herself with a big straw hat.

"I meant that in a good way."

This is how I always remember her best — summer Mema, drinking tea out on the porch, frying up okra, planting bulbs in the flower beds, and chasing off the rabbits with water from the hose. On our last night every August, I'd make Mom sleep on the couch so I could fall asleep holding Mema's hand. I never wanted to leave.

And then it hits me as I roll on back to the bedroom. I might never have to.

15
FISH FRIES AND PIE

All of us in Royal Oaks decide to caravan over to Bethlehem Methodist together. So at noon on the money, Mom and I pull into the church parking lot, followed by Mema and Grandpa in the Buick, and Susie, Dane, and Coralee in their old pickup. A minute later Mr. and Mrs. Akers and Bert pull in next to us.

The pie is on my lap, and I try to hold its covered dish tight and careful at the same time — like a goldfish in a bowl. I yelped at every bump on the way over until Mom said if I didn't calm down, she'd make the pie ride up in front with her.

It's a beauty of a day, cooler than I thought after spending all morning in the kitchen. When we get out, a breeze is blowing through the trees.

I threaten Mom with her life when I hand her the pie. I don't trust myself to hold it while I roll into the room where the contest is being held. I remember that this room is actually a gym. There are lines painted on the floor and basketball hoops all folded up into the ceiling. Today, though, it looks more like a farmers market or a circus.

Right in the middle at half-court, four long folding tables make a square. Their lacy tablecloths blow in the breeze from the big fans that have been wheeled in to keep out the heat and the flies.

"Oh, honey, nice to see a little baker out today!" It's Evelyn. She's standing inside the square of tables in a bright orange sleeveless dress and hat. She looks like a traffic cone.

"Here you go." She hands me a green sticker and a marker. "Put your name on this and stick it right to the bottom of your pie plate. This's so it stays anonymous."

She leans in. "We've had some incidents in the past," she says, then drops her voice to a whisper. "You know, of cheating." Her eyes go wide. "People were submitting more than one pie. We even had one of the judges try to sneak one in once."

I don't say anything, because what do you say to all that? And then she winks at me, so I'm not sure if she was kidding. But I write my name and stick it on the bottom of the pie dish anyway, just in case. I leave the pie cover on. I'm waiting for the big reveal — not even Mom knows what's under there.

It feels good to have the pie out of my hands. Now there's nothing to do but wait and see. I pray real quick and then cross my fingers, too, just to cover all my bases.

More folding tables have been set up all along the walls for the silent auction, and Bert and Coralee and I move down the line, weaving in and around the bidders to pass the time.

There are gift certificates to Church's Chicken and handmade dollhouses that open and close with a hinge. Quilts with sunflowers and pinwheels and grapevines hang from racks on the walls. There's even one made from old T-shirts.

Bert picks up a vintage camera, but the

man in charge of monitoring the tables takes it away from him when he almost drops it. In one corner somebody's actually parked a canoe, complete with paddles and life jackets.

There are iPads and flat-screens and laptops, too.

Methodists do not mess around with their auctions.

Coralee is holding up an old-fashioned house phone in the shape of a piano when we hear the dinner bell clang. It's an actual bell as big as a beach ball that they roll in once a year for the fish fry. I bet you can hear it all the way across the lake.

The line for catfish spills out into the parking lot. People at the back have to wave off the councilmen and councilwomen holding up signs and handing out stickers with their names printed on them.

By the time we get to the front, the men at the fryers are already sweating through their T-shirts, but they smile when I hand over my double-layered paper plate. I skip the coleslaw and beg extra fish and hush puppies. The plate is so hot on my lap, I have to hold it up and get Coralee and Bert to push me over to the picnic tables. They each take one handle and are basically terrible at walking together, so I feel a little carsick by the time we find everybody already sitting at a table under the oaks.

"How'd you get your food so fast?" I ask.

Nobody says anything.

"You cut in line, didn't you?" I say, and poke a fork at Mema. "You *cut in line* at a church function. Whatever happened to 'do unto thy neighbor'?"

She takes a long sip of sweet tea and says, "Honey, everybody knows that does not apply to a fish fry."

Mom snorts into her tea. She looks so beautiful that for a minute I put my fork down. She's wearing a white sleeveless dress, and her arms are freckled from the sun, and she's gained some weight since we've been here with all of Mema's cooking. She doesn't look so breakable.

I run my hands down my own legs. I'm in jean shorts today, and I squeeze my thighs a little. They're bigger, stronger maybe from all the exercises Hutch has me doing.

"How're y'all on this fine afternoon?"

It's like I magicked him here. Hutch sits down next to me and smiles at everybody. Mom smiles down into her lap.

Ten minutes of serious eating later and I'm so full I'm wishing my shorts were elastic. Coralee is lying on top of the picnic table, even though people are still hunting for spots. She's humming the national anthem and tapping her stomach to the beat.

"Bert," I call across the table.

"What?" He looks up from his phone. Half his siblings are about to come home for the summer, and they're all texting him like they've just remembered he exists.

"When do they announce the winner for the contest?" My stomach flutters underneath all the catfish.

"How should I know?"

"Your dad's the one offering the prize."

"Yeah, but he doesn't have anything to do with the contest. They won't even let him near the pies. They say his presence could influence the results."

I cannot believe how seriously they take this. I feel like I've entered the Pie Olympics.

"I'll go check, baby girl." Grandpa gets up. "I think they're about done with the next batch anyway," he says, nodding toward the catfish fryers.

Mema shakes her head. "That man could eat a horse."

"Hey, you want to play horseshoes?" Coralee says, and I nod, because I'll do anything to keep from thinking about the contest. We take Bert's phone away and drag him with us.

"You cheated!"

"Coralee, I did not. There is no possible way to cheat at horseshoes."

"Yes, there is, Bert. I saw you step over that line."

"It doesn't matter anyway. Ellie's still winning."

I only half hear them. It's been ten minutes and still no Grandpa. I leave them to it and go back over to the picnic tables. Our place is now taken up by a family with a stroller, and I can't see Mom or Mema anywhere.

I roll back into the gym. Maybe they're bidding on the silent auction. But it's so hot in there, I can't stay more than a minute or two. Just long enough to see they're not in there.

I'm about to go back to the horseshoes when Mom comes running.

"Ellie, we've got to go." She takes me by the handles.

"Hey, no! What are you doing? They haven't even announced the winner yet!"

We're wheeling toward the parking lot so fast, the wind's whipping my hair.

"You grandfather's gone. He took the Buick."

"What?"

But I see Mema already in the front seat of the van and motioning out the window for us to hurry up.

Nobody says a word as we speed toward home.

Our street is quiet. There's not even a dog barking. It seems like the whole world went down to church today.

The Buick's not in the drive.

Mema starts to cry.

Mom turns around in her seat to look at me. "Ellie, I need you to stay here."

"Mom, no —"

"Hush now. I need you here in case Grandpa comes back or somebody calls the house phone. Can you do that for me?"

She's already out of the van and lowering the lift. So I just nod. I'm too scared to do anything else. I'm barely out and on the front walk when they back down the driveway in a cloud of dust.

I know I'm supposed to go into the house, but it's too quiet. I can't sit still. I rock back and forth in place. I tilt back and look at the blue, blue sky cut in half by the telephone wire. Somewhere up in the tree, a bird caws. It sounds like a crow. I drop back down and roll along the front walk, bumping over the seashells Mema put down in the cement after their one trip to the beach. I stop by the canning shed and sit in the shade. I try not to panic.

That's when I hear it.

A humming.

It's coming from the garage, but nobody ever uses the garage for parking. It's always been used to hold mowers and oilcans and garden tools. And Grandpa's woodworking. I shiver in the shade and roll forward, put my ear to the door real slowly. I can hear it better now, though I still can't tell what it is. It's kind of like a soft purr.

I bang on the metal door, and it's so loud I scare myself. Nobody answers. I lean all the way down and grab the handle and try to pull. The door is so heavy, it lifts only an inch or two. But out from that inch drifts a cloud of car fumes that makes me turn and cough.

I bang and bang on the door until my palm's on fire. I lock my wheelchair in place and use both hands to grab at the handle and lift. Each time I can only get it cracked. Grandpa's in there, I know it.

And I can't get to him.

I can't stop crying.

I call Mom.

She doesn't answer.

I leave a message that is just me crying.

"Grandpa!" I ram the door with my chair and almost tip over. But it's enough to knock it up and get it moving, and I pull and pull. The skin's ripping off my hands. It doesn't matter. The door is up.

It's up and I'm coughing in a cloud of exhaust. The Buick's in there, but I can't get the chair between it and the wall. Up in front, Grandpa sits slumped over the wheel like he's fallen asleep.

16

Buoyed

Dear Mrs. Julia Child,

Google just told me you are no longer alive, but I had it in my mind to write you a thank-you, and so I'm going to do it anyway, because I need something to do with my hands.

I am writing to thank you for your recipe for piecrust. I found it in my mom's copy of Mastering the Art of French Cooking. At first my grandma said French cooking was too snooty, but when she found out it had shortening in it, she said, "Anything that uses Crisco is okay by me."

Somebody close to me told me that if I was going to make a prizewinning pie, I had to pick something that spoke to me.

The problem is a lot of things speak

to me. I like fancy French food and also biscuits and gravy and chocolate-dipped cones from Dairy Queen and miniature golf and sudoku (thanks to my grandma).

So I decided to make a pie that would speak to every part of me. I used your crust because it's nice and sweet and a little fancy, and I used blackberries my grandma and I picked from her garden and canned last summer, because it's still spring here and I thought people would like a taste of what's ahead. And I glazed it all in lemon because lemon is my grandpa's favorite and I wanted to make him smile.

So I guess this is a letter to my family, too, for helping me make the best blackberry lemon pie in the whole of Eufaula. I can say that for real because I have a blue ribbon and a hundred-dollar grocery certificate to prove it.

Many thanks,
Ellie

It's too dark in this room. I don't know why it always has to be too dark or too bright or too cold or too hot. But I guess you don't come to the hospital for a good night's sleep.

Mom and Mema are down in the family room meeting with the doctors. I told them I'd keep an eye on Grandpa. Not that he's going anywhere. I can hear his breathing, steady and calm, and that makes me calm. I've never been in this position before — the visitor in the hospital.

After we got to the ER, the paramedics said I was a hero. They said if I hadn't busted open that garage door, it could have been much worse. They didn't say worse how. They didn't need to.

I lay my head on Grandpa's knee and shut my eyes. My hands itch where the nurse bandaged up the cuts. It feels like a lifetime and a day since baking in the kitchen this morning with Coralee.

I feel a hand on my head.

"Hey, stop that crying now."

"Grandpa!" I sit up and grab at his hand with my own. It's purple and veiny, and I'm careful not to touch the IV. "You're supposed to be resting."

"Well, I think this counts." He coughs and smiles. "Hey, now. I said no crying. I'm gonna be okay."

And he looks okay. A little pale maybe, and his voice is hoarse. Otherwise, he looks normal. But I can't help thinking, *That's the problem, isn't it? He* always *looks normal.* I squeeze his hand.

"What's my name?"

"What?" He looks confused for a second, and I hate it, but I have to ask.

"Just — what's my name?"

"Dolly Parton."

"That's not funny."

"Honey, I know you're Ellie. But I don't blame you."

He coughs, and I scoot closer.

"Grandpa, why'd you run off like that?"

"Well, it's kind of a funny story," he says, and laughs, but I can't. "I went to check on the contest, like I told you. Then when I got in there and saw all the trinkets at the silent auction, I remembered I'd left my own at home, the woodworking I'd been doing. I thought I'd just drive on home to fetch it."

He stops talking, and I think that's the end of it, and I want to ask, *Why, why did you park in the garage? Why did you shut the door? Why didn't you turn the car off?* but he's rubbing his eyes and there's a little blood on his hand from where they had to stick him twice with the needle for the IV. So I decide to leave it for now.

I'm about to push the button for the nurse when he says, "Ellie, I guess I just got a little confused, is all."

"Oh, Grandpa."

"Ellie, I know I'm not right some of the time." He picks at some dirt under his thumbnail, like a little kid. "But most of the time I am, honey, and that's just a hard line to walk."

"They're talking about making you live somewhere else."

I didn't mean to say it, didn't mean to tattle. But he doesn't look surprised.

"I know, baby. Your grandma and I have been discussing it."

"But I don't want you to leave!"

I yell so loud a nurse comes by and

shushes me and then sees Grandpa is awake and goes off to fetch a doctor.

"Honey, it's not like they're dumping me at a street corner and going on their merry way. Some of the places we've looked at are mighty fine, nicer than our trailer, that's for sure. And your grandma would come with me. We'd even get a little space to do some gardening."

"I like our trailer."

"I know you do."

And then I pull out my blue ribbon and hand it to him. Evelyn drove by the hospital just to give it to me. He holds it up to the light like he's looking at a gemstone.

"Well, I'll be. First place."

"And a hundred dollars to boot."

"That's my girl."

He's closing his eyes now, and I think I ought to let him rest, but I want to ask one last thing.

"Grandpa?"

"What, honey?"

"What'd you go back for? For the auction, I mean. What'd you make?"

He opens his eyes and looks at me.

"It was a mailbox in the shape of a pie. I guess I had you on my mind."

Before we leave that night, I tape the ribbon to the foot of his bed, so he'll see it first thing when he wakes up and remember.

One day during the summer when I was nine, Grandpa had been promising me all morning we'd go fishing. It would be the first time out on the boat that season. It was ninety degrees at noon, but I was in my chair waiting by the van right after lunch.

"Honey, you don't have to wear that life vest until we hit the water," he said as we backed down the drive.

"I know."

I left it on because how can you explain to a grown-up how it feels to be so close to the thing you've been waiting for? But when we got to the dock and were backing the boat down into the water, the clouds swooped in with a flash summer storm. It was thundering and dark as night and we had to turn around.

I cried all the way home.

I was sitting in my chair watching reruns of *The Magic School Bus* when Mema came in. She was holding out an umbrella.

"Your grandpa's got a surprise for you."

I didn't want to go, but she wheeled me out into the rain anyway and down the gravel driveway to the carport next to the garage. Grandpa was standing by an old trash can, and flames rose up out of it and licked the sides.

Without a word, he passed me a coat hanger he'd unbent and helped me stick a hot dog on the end of it. His apron said WORLD'S WORST CHEF.

We sat out there all afternoon roasting hot dogs and playing cards while the yard filled with puddles, and Mom and Mema watched from the porch.

"Sometimes," Grandpa said when it finally stopped raining and the sun came out, "the best plan is the one you don't make for yourself."

Dear Dad,
    I can't believe you got me the cookie

scooper! I know it's not super fancy and doesn't look like much, but I have made a million cookies a million times faster, and it's awesome! So thank you!

And yes, when you come to visit this summer, I promise to make the oatmeal raisin cookies.

Ellie

June in Oklahoma is like living on the sun. Or at least that's what it feels like in the bed of the pickup as it bounces down the road to No. 9 landing.

"You know we'd get arrested for this in Nashville," I yell through the open window into the cab of the truck. I'm in the back with Bert and Coralee in a nest of life vests and inner tubes.

"Good thing we moved, then!" Mom yells back.

Coralee laughs and slaps Bert on the back so hard he drops his phone. "What in the world has gotten into your mother?" she shouts toward me, her hair whipping free from her ponytail.

I shrug and look up at Mom. Her

sunglasses are pushed up into her hair, which is crazier looking than ever now that she's growing it out again. Hutch follows us in the van with my chair and enough Gatorade and chips and watermelon to last us all summer.

It's not even ten in the morning when we get to the lake, and we have it all to ourselves. Hutch puts me in my chair in the shade while everybody unloads. The sky is wavy with heat and I'm sticky with sweat. I lift my thighs up from where they're suctioned to the chair.

It's perfect.

"All right." Mom kneels down in front of me and rubs a fifth coat of sunscreen onto my shoulders. "Are you sure about this?"

"Mom."

"Ellie."

"If you back out now, I will fire you. I will fire you as my mother."

"Well, good luck to you, then," she says, and starts to get up.

"Come on!"

I can see Coralee and Bert standing

with their feet already in the water.

"Okay, okay. Just promise me you'll be careful."

"Okay, yes, I promise."

She wheels me over the wet sand right up to the edge of the lake. Hutch is waiting there, and he bends down and tightens the straps on my life jacket and the floaties on my arms and legs.

"Ready, Ellie?" he says.

"Ready."

And then he lifts me out of the chair and walks into the water.

The lake's still cool this early in the summer, and my skin is so hot that the shock of it gives me goose bumps. Once we're deep enough, he lowers me all the way in and I lie back with my arms out.

Coralee and Bert swim up to me on either side. Coralee's hair is so bright in the sun, it looks white, and Bert is a pale ghost in the muddy water.

"Okay, you can let go now."

"Are you sure?"

"Hutch, let go."

After a second he does. And I let the

water take me. My body floats weightless, each part as steady and strong as the rest.

I kick a little with my foot and practice moving one leg and then the other, until I am moving out farther from the shore.

I lift my head and see Mom standing with her hands on her hips.

I wave.

She waves back.

When I reach the buoys that separate the swimming area from the rest of the lake, I see they are orange and faded in the sun. I grab onto one, and Bert and Coralee each take another. A fish swims by and brushes up against my leg, and then it must reach Coralee, because she screams, and we're all laughing, and the sun isn't so hot now.

Mom and I are going over to Grandpa and Mema's condo for supper. I've promised to bring dessert. They're at Autumn Leaves now. There's a fitness center and an indoor swimming pool and a community garden and poker night, and I think they might like it better than the trailer, which is okay because the trailer is ours now and they can still come visit all the time. And once Mom gets settled into her permanent teaching job at the high school, she promises a full renovation *with* a handicapped shower. The pie mailbox is already up.

After a few minutes I turn around and close my eyes and let go of the buoy and drift. *Wherever you want to take me,* I think as the waves pull me along.

I hear Coralee yelling, "Hey, wait for us!" but my ears are underwater and it comes to me gently.

I am floating.

ACKNOWLEDGMENTS

To Reka Simonsen, my editor: Your enthusiasm for this project and your belief in Ellie's voice proved it wasn't all in my head — there really was magic here. You also managed to ferret out all the words I play on repeat. I will probably do it again, so this is both "Thank you" and "I'm sorry."

And to my agent, Keely Boeving, who received the first emails and frantic texts about this project. Thank you for finding the giant potholes in the early drafts and helping me scoop some plot in there. You are my left brain. Also, thank you for being agent, editor, and friend. I am three times blessed.

Thank you also to my children, the little people who make me my most imaginative self. Charlie, you are a beam of sunlight. People want to curl up near you, me included. That wheelchair has never stopped you, and I can't believe my luck that I get to be your mom. Jonas, if you want to be Jupiter when you grow up, go for it, buddy. And Cora, when you rule the world, please remember your mother, who never made you wear a bow and always let you read as late into the night as you wanted.

Jody, you get my Owen Meany THANK-YOU in all caps, because that's how grateful I am to be married to you and to raise our crazy family together. I swear we will go to Greece one day.

I'd also like to thank Deb Perelman and Mary Berry, my very favorite chefs. You helped me bake my way through a great many internal and external crises. Because of you, my family is well fed and so is my psyche.

To KJ Dell'Antonia and Jess Lahey, brilliant writers and podcasters extraordinaire: Thank you for your wisdom and wit and everything in between on #amwriting. It's the best podcast in the land.

And Kristin Tubb, thank you for liking the first pages of that *other* book enough to read this one. You have a kind and generous heart. Here's to more coffee dates in our future.

Lastly, I want to acknowledge the children, one in seven, living with a dis-ability. You are all forces to be reckoned with and wonderfully made. You are fighters, and I am honored to write this story for you.

ABOUT THE AUTHOR

Jamie Sumner's work has appeared in *The New York Times, The Washington Post,* and other publications. She loves stories that celebrate the grit and beauty in all kids and is the author of the middle grade novel *Roll with It.* She is also the mother to a son with cerebral palsy and lives with her family in Nashville, Tennessee. Visit her at Jamie-Sumner.com

The employees of Thorndike Press hope you have enjoyed this Large Print book. All our Thorndike, Wheeler, and Kennebec Large Print titles are designed for easy reading, and all our books are made to last. Other Thorndike Press Large Print books are available at your library, through selected bookstores, or directly from us.

For information about titles, please call:
  (800) 223-1244

or visit our website at:
  gale.com/thorndike

To share your comments, please write:
  Publisher
  Thorndike Press
  10 Water St., Suite 310
  Waterville, ME 04901